BULL AND OTHER STORIES

Bull and Other Stories

Kathy Anderson

Autumn House Press receives state arts funding support through a grant from the Pennsylvania Council on the Arts, a state agency funded by the Commonwealth of Pennsylvania, and the National Endowment for the Arts, a federal agency.

ISBN: 978-1-938769-11-5
Library of Congress Control Number: 2015954118

All Autumn House books are printed on acid-free paper and meet the international standards for permanent books intended for purchase by libraries.

For my wife, Jackie Warren

Grateful acknowledgment is made for permission to reprint the following:

"(How Much is That) Doggie in the Window" Written by Bob Merrill
Copyright 1952, Renewed 1980 Golden Bell Songs

"You Are So Beautiful"
Words and Music by Billy Preston and Bruce Fisher
Copyright © 1973 IRVING MUSIC, INC., and ALMO MUSIC CORP.
Copyright Renewed
All Rights Reserved. Used by Permission
Reprinted by Permission of Hal Leonard Corporation

CONTENTS

BULL AND OTHER STORIES

Bull

His father was now his mother but he was still an epic asshole.

"He won't even let me get a tattoo," Josh said. "He gets his whole dick cut off and he won't even let me get a tattoo."

Josh hated being forced to sit here at family therapy every week, the therapist and his parents waiting for him to miraculously be okay with the fact that his asshole father was now his asshole second mother or something. What a freak show.

"Call me Goat Boy," Josh said. "From this day forth, my name is Goat Boy. If he can change from a man to a woman, from Joe to Heidi, then I can do the same. I am officially changing my name to Goat Boy and my gender to half goat, half boy."

"I'm not paying good money for you to mutilate your body with tattoos like all the other losers," Heidi said.

"But you can mutilate your body and we're supposed to be all happy for you," Josh said.

"We're not here to talk about tattoos, Josh."

"Goat Boy."

"There's no such thing. But there is such a thing as a woman born into a man's body. We've been through this. You're fourteen, not some baby," said Heidi. She patted and stroked her long hair as she talked.

He looks stupid patting his hair like that. He stinks at this. Josh pictured Ashlee in his Spanish class, the sexy way she tugged on her ponytail when she smiled at him. Now that was how a real girl handled her hair. He felt an immediate erection rise up and gathered his coat over his lap to cover it.

"Maa-maa. Maa-maa. Goat Boy is bleating," Josh said.

"Knock it off, Josh," said his mother, Sue Ann. "It's not easy for me either but you don't see me bleating."

"Maa-maa, I was born into a goat body and you'll just have to accept me as I am," Josh said. "If I have to accept him as a she-male, he has to accept me as a goat boy. Maa-maa."

"She-male is not an acceptable way to describe Heidi, Josh," the therapist said.

"Josh is not an acceptable way to address Goat Boy," Josh said.

"Heidi is still the same person," the therapist said. "I'd like you to try something, Josh. Just for a minute. Turn your whole body toward Heidi and look her right in the eyes."

Josh turned his whole body to face his father. He looked him right in the eyes and held his gaze for a full minute, forcing himself to wait before he spoke.

He felt sick at what he saw. He wasn't used to it at all, even though his father had started dressing like a woman months before his surgeries. It was still disgusting and wrong and ugly. His father had been a regular looking man, kind of nerdy, with square glasses and a normal dad haircut. He had been a skinny guy, clean-shaven always. He said he couldn't stand the scruffy look that so many movie stars and singers had. *They look dirty with that stubble on their faces*, he had said. *Look at that bum, why would it be a fashion to look like a dirty bum.*

Now Josh saw the strangest man when he looked at his father. Puffy face. Long straight blonde hair. Red lipstick! Eyes ringed with brown eyeliner, fluttering long eyelashes. Contact lenses instead of glasses. He didn't know how to dress like a woman. Nothing fit him right. His blouse was all bunchy and his skirt started way high above his waist and hung below his knees, like it belonged on an old nun. To Josh, he looked like he was in a cheap Halloween costume or like he was one of those gross female impersonator guys in the Philadelphia Mummers Parade strutting down the street with big red lips and a ruffled umbrella. He was a fake woman with fake breasts and a fake vagina and nothing would change that.

There was a family story about the first time Josh saw his dad's penis, but Josh was too young to actually remember. He had heard his mom tell the story to girlfriends cackling around the kitchen table and to tipsy aunts at family parties. His dad had been trying to teach Josh to pee in the toilet while standing up. Toddler Josh looked at his dad's penis, pointed to it, and said one of the few words he knew, "big." Josh wished he didn't have a picture of that story in his mind. He would give anything to be able to take a penknife to his brain and cut it away.

Josh saw an eager look on his dad's face, like he was waiting to hear a compliment. Like he actually thought Josh would be one molecule of okay with this. Fuck that shit.

"Hey Dad, how are you doing in there? You can come out now. Admit it was all a crazy mistake. Take off the makeup and stockings, chop off that hair, stop taking hormones because that's a losing battle. Hate to break it to you, Dad, but you still look like a dude. Your big feet and hands—dead giveaway. What are you going to do—chop them off too? I don't think so. Period, end of story," Josh said.

His dad looked away, his face reddening. Josh felt his heart thumping like a drummer was flailing wildly around on his rib cage. He wanted to ask his mother if she was going to stay married to this asshole. Did she even want to be married to a woman? She didn't sign up for this. Poor Mom.

"Can we wrap this up?" Sue Ann said. "I've had about as much of this as I can take for one day."

"We have ten more minutes on the clock," Heidi said.

"Un. Fucking. Believable. He wants to get his money's worth," Josh said.

"Why do you let him dominate these sessions?" Heidi said to the therapist. "It's outrageous. Everything is not about him."

"I said I'm done, Joe," Sue Ann said. "I mean Heidi." It was the same voice she used to order Josh and the farm animals around. No nonsense.

Josh loved when his mom cracked. When she called him Joe. When she said "my husband." It meant he wasn't the only one who looked at Heidi and still saw Joe in there.

"I have my own money," Josh said. "I'm getting a tattoo with my own money."

In the front seat of the truck, his parents exchanged a look. It was too fast. He couldn't tell what was going on up there.

"It's not about the money," Sue Ann said. "We don't want you to do something you'll be sorry about later in life."

"Like you never did that."

"Yeah, we did stupid shit, Josh," Sue Ann said. "So we feel like that's our job, to save you from doing stupid shit, all right? Enough. Get off it."

Josh felt a rage so huge he wanted to pound his fists against the truck windows and break out of there like Superman, roar out into the corn fields and knock down everything in his path—barns, cows, fences, tractors—smash it all down.

"I hate you," he cried. "You suck. I don't know why I was even born. Do you know what kind of shit I have to endure every day of my life, having a she-male for a father? Do you know what happens to me at school every day? Anyone else would have blown their brains out by now. And all I ask is one thing. I want a fucking tattoo on my arm. And I am getting one, no matter what you say or do. If I have to go to an illegal place where they don't ask for the stinking permission form because I'm underage, I will. And if I die from an infection because you made me go to a butcher tattoo shop, that's fine. I'll be better off dead anyway."

His parents looked at each other again. They did that thing married people do, talk with their eyes. Josh hated when they did that. It wasn't fair to send thoughts to each other instead of having to say them out loud so he could hear.

Finally Sue Ann said, "We said get off it, Josh." But her voice wavered and Josh knew that meant his parents were weakening.

"All you care about is yourselves. You don't even care what I go through. I have a right to my own life. I have a right to get a tattoo. It's my body. Luke got a tattoo when he was eleven. Stevie got his first one when he was twelve and now he has like ten of them all over him. All my friends have tattoos. I'm the only one without one." He wasn't going to bring up Ashlee, who had a purple rose tattoo on her lower back and a pierced belly button.

"We'll talk about it later," Heidi said finally. She still drove like a guy, one arm draped over the top of the steering wheel.

"There is no later," Josh said.

"What's that supposed to mean?" Sue Ann said.

"I'm doing it this weekend. Or else."

"You don't speak to us like that," Sue Ann said. "You don't tell us what to do and when." But she didn't sound like herself. She sounded like a new mom, who was not quite sure of what she was supposed to say. His normal mom was a bellower. When she yelled at you, you moved. She got lots of practice yelling at the cows, who were good at getting out of the pasture and milling around in the middle of the road. When she yelled at the pigs, they jerked around and followed her.

"I'm not telling you what to do. I'm telling you what I'm going to do. This weekend."

Everything Josh had said about school was a lie. His friends were great. They said the right thing when they heard about his dad. They said they were sorry. It was like a dad dying, wasn't it? Like what you say to a guy whose dad dies. Sorry for your loss.

Just one guy gave him a hard time. Bernardo wanted to be a filmmaker and he would not shut up about making a documentary about Joe/Heidi. Every time Josh saw Bernardo coming, he ran. He was sick of hearing how important the film project was, how it would go viral, how Josh would be famous for having a tranny dad. He hated the stupid questions Bernardo kept asking. *What exactly did they do with his dick after they cut it off? Does he keep it in a jar like my uncle's kidney stones? Is he a lesbian now, because he's still married to your mom?* Bernardo said, *Don't you see, it's like a story of America, here in lower Delaware, all these farms and shit, and there's your dad, walking in a corn field with her long blond hair blowing in the wind, no city around him to protect him, nobody else like him.*

His friends said they would lean on Bernardo to shut him up, if Josh wanted. But Josh said no. He was trying to keep a low profile. If he got in trouble at school, those fucking family therapy sessions might go on forever.

The tattoo guy was a girl. Josh didn't expect that. She was covered with tattoos herself, her arms and legs a sea of colors and pictures. She looked like a cartoon that you wanted to read, with a story line that led you up one arm and down her back, down her leg and up her other arm.

She barely glanced at his forged permission form and didn't even ask him for i.d. Josh could not believe his good luck. He actually thought they would throw him right out the front door and tell him to come back in a few years.

She didn't look directly at him, but gestured for him to sit down in her chair and stood over him silently.

"I want a real big one," he said. He pulled out a picture of a huge bull with red angry eyes and black flared nostrils. It was an intricate beautiful design, with curly plumes of smoke coming out of the bull's nose and his legs kicking up in the air. "On my right arm. Like I want his tail to end up in my armpit and the rest of him all over my whole arm. And when I move my arm, can it look like the bull is pawing on the ground?"

"Jesus Christ," she said. "I knew it. I knew someone would ask for something really, really hard on my first day. I might as well quit right now. I'm sorry, man." Her face scrunched up and her eyes filled with tears.

"Don't be sorry. I'm sorry. I didn't mean to ask for something hard," Josh said.

"I don't know what to do anymore. Everything I touch turns to total crap. I try so hard," she cried.

Josh felt totally helpless. He didn't know what to do or say to make her stop. He stood up.

"It's okay. I don't even need it. I can go," Josh said.

"No. No. No," she said. "I have to do this. I can't keep fucking up my whole entire useless life."

"Are you sure? I'm cool with not doing it. I swear," Josh said.

"Fake it till you make it. Fake it till you make it," she chanted under her breath. Her hands shook as she groped for her tattoo gun.

Josh turned around, reached out, and touched her hand with one finger. He was trying to settle her down, the way he laid his hands softly on the farm animals when they were scared. When it was time to inseminate the heifers, he was the one who stroked their backs to keep them calm and held the tail up in the air while his mom reached deep inside them to thread the insemination rod into the uterus and pump the bull semen in. He had the magic touch, his mom said.

The tattoo girl still didn't look him in the eyes but she opened her palm and took his hand, breathing heavily like she was trying to catch her breath. She held on tight, like she was bobbing in choppy water and he was her lifeline.

He was so happy holding her hand. He had forgotten what happy felt like. It was like he just ate a warm, oozy brownie where the taste stayed in his mouth and filled him up everywhere. It was like waking up after a wonderful dream where a girl put her mouth right on his penis and her soft long hair fell all over his naked body. Wow.

The tattoo girl whispered, "You're a good guy, you know that? Thanks for being so super nice to me."

"It's nothing. Everyone should always be nice to you all the time. Don't even worry about it. You won't be nervous forever. It's only your first day," Josh said.

"Come here, you," she said, pulling him close. She hugged him so fiercely and for so long that he almost fainted with pleasure. She smelled so incredibly good. "Let's try again. I think I'm ready now."

Josh smiled and sat down in her tattoo chair. He took off his shirt, hoping he didn't smell of cows or sweat. She studied his picture, made a stencil of the bull, then wiped his arm and armpit with rubbing alcohol. The gentle way she swabbed him down and the feel of her hands on him were so wonderful that he had to stop himself from laughing out loud.

When the first stab of the needle in the tattoo gun landed under his armpit, Josh cried out in shock. It felt like the needle reached all the way to his bone, like she was stabbing him with a jagged knife, ripping him open. Was this normal? Or was he a baby who couldn't stand a little pain?

She continued, panting a little and murmuring under her breath, like she was remembering the steps and repeating them to herself. She stabbed so hard and so fast, Josh couldn't even find words to stop her. The pain paralyzed him. Finally his nose started gushing blood and he vomited and fainted almost at the exact same time. As he slid from the chair to the floor, he saw the air turn a gorgeous shimmering green all around him. *Isn't that amazing, there's all this green hidden under the air*, was his last thought before blacking out.

Someday he would tell his wife about the first woman who got under his skin. He would describe it all—the bull, the green cloud that enveloped him, the ink that remained under his armpit in a trail that went nowhere. How that was the moment he knew his childhood was over. He would tell his wife he was born into his manhood covered with blood and vomit and paralyzed by pain. Try having a baby claw its way out of you and then we'll talk, she would say, laughing.

When Josh woke up in the emergency room and saw two faces looming over him, his first thought was, *Who's that lady with my mom?* Then he saw Heidi reach her long, hairy arm with her big man's hands around his mom's shoulder and he knew. He closed his eyes again, but he could feel her there, waiting.

GO. STOP.

"EVERYONE IS getting cancer," Gina said, pointing her cigarette at her boyfriend Morrison. They were walking her dog PrettyBoy, a hairy, little beast with bulgy eyes and gaping nostrils. Every time Gina puffed on her cigarette, PrettyBoy snorted dramatically, like he was saying *Knock off the fumes, bitch*.

"Who's getting cancer?" Morrison asked.

"Everyone is getting cancer," she said. "The dogs are getting cancer, the artists are getting cancer, the cheerleaders are getting cancer, the stepdads are getting cancer, the babies are getting cancer, the queers are getting cancer, the roofers are getting cancer, the bikers are getting cancer. Everyone is getting cancer."

"That's ridiculous. Everyone is not getting cancer."

"I'm telling you. Everyone is getting cancer." Gina stomped her feet on the sidewalk, stopped walking, and turned to face Morrison.

PrettyBoy sighed and rolled his eyes. The dog park was right there. PrettyBoy could practically touch it. They were on Chestnut Street. Next was Front Street and the dog park, with its view of the Delaware River. They had just passed the Irish Memorial at the edge of the park, a huge gray sculpture mound depicting multitudes of dead Irish people from the famine years and those fleeing to America on disease-ridden ships.

"I don't have it. You don't have it."

"Yet."

"So what can we do about it anyway?"

"Move."

"Move where?"

"Where they don't have cancer."

"Where's that, never-never land?"

Gina whipped out her phone and tapped a search into it. "Nepal. Yemen. Mauritania."

"I like the sound of that, Mauritania. Sounds watery, oceanic. Let's move there."

Gina read on. "They have slavery, female genital mutilation, and people live on less than $1.25 a day."

Now Morrison searched along with her, a smartphone duel. "Would you rather die of diarrhea, malaria, or AIDS? Chances are if we moved to Mauritania, that's what you'd die of instead."

"I hate the internet. It tells you everything and nothing. Not how to live your life. Not how to save your life," Gina said.

"One interesting fact . . ." Morrison said.

"Don't start," she answered, flinging her cigarette to the sidewalk and twisting her boot on it. "If I'm going to die of cancer anyway, I might as well enjoy a few lovely cigs along the way."

PrettyBoy barked three sharp snippy *arfs*, like he was saying *Hey, remember me?*

Gina picked PrettyBoy up, kissed his nose, and laid her cheek alongside his. "I love you, I love you, I love you so much, my PrettyBoy," she murmured into his ear. He smelled of the coconut oil shampoo and conditioner Gina used on him to keep his fur soft and sweet.

"More than me?" Morrison asked.

"You know that. He's the love of my life. My sole reason for being. I moved here because I knew he would be happy here."

Their Old City neighborhood was full of bars serving retro cocktails in restored old banks, chic hair salons, art galleries, and tiny shops selling artisanal stuff. But they weren't here for all that. They were here for the two dog parks that PrettyBoy loved, the one next to Christ Church, the oldest church in the city; and the one near the Delaware River, where you could see New Jersey on the other side. When PrettyBoy just needed to get out of the house and sniff a few butts, they went to yappy hour at Christ Church. When he needed to run like hell, they headed to the Irish Memorial park near the river.

"Geez, you know how to make a guy feel bad," Morrison said. He patted PrettyBoy's head.

"If you can't handle the heat, get out of the kitchen, mister," Gina said. "Stop changing the subject. Cancer."

"What's there to say? Life plays out the way it will." Morrison felt tremendous at the moment. He was able to touch Gina whenever he wanted, which was all the time. He wanted to bury his face in her hair, just like she did to PrettyBoy. And stay there forever, breathing her in. What a woman.

Gina put PrettyBoy down and they resumed walking. PrettyBoy panted loudly, inhaling the magnificent perfume of the dog park coming closer every second.

"People act like if they go on those stupid cancer walks and give money to cancer organizations when people die, that's going to help. All it does is throw gas on the fire to keep the cancer biz going. Those organizations are like master magicians distracting people," she said.

"Gina. Come on, babe. I'd like to enjoy a few minutes with you this morning before I have to go to work. Can you please . . .?"

Gina opened the dog park gates and leaned down to let PrettyBoy off his leash. He yelped joyfully and took off running as fast as his stumpy legs could run.

"The truth is there are huge companies making a shitload of money off cancer." She pointed her finger into Morrison's chest. He grabbed it and held on.

"There's agribusiness genetically modifying our food. There's the chemical industry injecting pesticides and chemicals into our land, our water, our air. We eat shit. We breathe shit. We drink shit. That's why everyone is getting cancer. There's no mystery. We don't need to raise money to search for this mysterious cause. We need to stop poisoning people to death," she said.

He stuck her finger in his mouth. She smiled and he bit down lightly.

Gina and Morrison watched PrettyBoy tear around the dog park, jumping on other dogs' backs and head-butting them until they chased him back. Round and round the pack of dogs went—a whirl of ChowHound, Peterkins, PeanutChew, Sherlock, Spotty, CrayCray, LadyAnne, and Sukie—led by PrettyBoy, grinning his fool head off.

Ten blocks away, Mr. and Mrs. James G. Huddleston slowly climbed into their 1975 Cadillac Seville, at one time a shiny Georgian silver but now mostly rust-colored from many dents, scratches, and holes.

Mr. Huddleston's eyes and ears didn't work anymore. After a botched eye operation, he was actually a one-eyed man now and that one eye did not see colors like green and red, only hazy gray fog.

He refused to stop driving, however, and did not believe that any of the dents, scratches, and holes were his fault. The other drivers in this city were all crazy. He was careful. His doctor, who was required by law to report him to the Department of Transportation if he did not appear capable of safe driving, advised him not to drive and asked him to consider the innocent people he could hurt if he did drive. Mr. Huddleston was ninety-one, after all. Mr. Huddleston swore to the doctor that Mrs. Huddleston drove them everywhere. In fact, she had never driven a car in her life.

Mrs. Huddleston could still see colors. When they drove, her job was to call out "Red light. STOP." And "Green light. GO." But Mr. Huddleston, who was quite deaf, often could not hear her shouting at him. And Mrs. Huddleston's voice was getting softer by the minute, so she couldn't always raise her voice loud enough to get through to Mr. Huddleston. But still they drove their two-ton car around the city of Philadelphia because they couldn't walk anymore. Their legs were too shaky to hold them up. The Huddlestons fell down if they didn't have chairs and tables to hold on to, inching their way around their house like toddlers learning to walk.

Today they were going on a very sad journey in their formerly elegant, now rattletrap car. The Huddlestons were going to the funeral of one of their oldest friends, Georgina Jackson, who had only been eighty-five years old when she fell out of her nursing home bed, cracked her skull wide open, and died.

The funeral was in New Jersey, on the other side of the Ben Franklin Bridge. This was causing Mr. Huddleston tremendous anxiety. He had not driven so far in two decades, but he was determined that they would attend Georgina's funeral.

If they didn't, he feared no one would be there. Georgina had no close family and few friends left. He thought of her wild red hair and her exuberant laugh and how they had run into the ocean together for so many summers down the Jersey shore, the waves moving their bodies up and down in exhilarating rhythm. The same families and couples vacationed together year after year, renting adjacent small houses. Who remembered now how it had started? Did the families know each other before the shore days or had they all met on the beach and vowed to return for the same weeks every year? He thought of the night Georgina and he had met on the beach after everyone else was asleep and how they fell on each other like animals. Only once, but it had meant everything to Mr. Huddleston.

"We could take a cab," said Mrs. Huddleston.

"We are not taking a cab," said Mr. Huddleston. "We have a perfectly good car."

"But the doctor . . ."

"He's an ass."

It was not too late to climb out of the car and hail a cab. Mr. Huddleston hesitated. Mrs. Huddleston put her hand on his arm. This small timid act enraged him. How dare she tell him what to do. She's got another think coming if she thinks he will ever listen to her bossing him around. He started the car.

"If I get it," Gina said. "I'm not getting treatment. I'm going to sell everything I own, pack up PrettyBoy, and go see the world."

"I'm coming with you," Morrison said. "I'll follow you to the ends of the earth."

"Good," Gina said. "I'll need someone to take care of PrettyBoy after I'm gone. You'll do."

"You're so hard," Morrison said, his hand sliding under her sweater. "You won't give me an inch."

Gina laughed and wiggled herself close to him. She backed up, feeling his arms wrap around her and his chin rest on her head.

"I give you plenty of inches," she said.

PrettyBoy and Sukie, his best dog friend, ran up and plopped down by Gina and Morrison, resting.

The Huddlestons lurched forward. Mrs. Huddleston clutched the door handle with both of her trembling hands. Mr. Huddleston waited for the voice to tell him what to do. "GO. STOP. GO. STOP." For eight blocks, they carried on like this. Because they were traveling so slowly, walkers and bicyclists were able to dodge the Huddlestons zigzagging down the street, although a few of them banged their fists on the car after near misses. Every time he heard the fists banging on metal, Mr. Huddleston thought of baked potatoes falling from the sky like hail and landing on his car. He loved baked potatoes. He wished they would bounce right in his car window and land in his lap. He was starving. Nothing tasted good anymore. His teeth ached so badly and his stomach hurt all the time.

Mrs. Huddleston's heart was thumping alarmingly and she couldn't catch her breath. *I can't go on*, she thought. *He is the most stubborn jackass that ever walked on this Earth.* She knew why he was so determined to go to this funeral. His fling with that trashy redhead was no secret to her. Georgina couldn't keep a secret like that. She was proud of seducing men, especially married men. Part of Georgina's fun was letting it slip out and watching the wives react. Georgina had seduced most of the men in their social circle and had broken up quite a few marriages. Mrs. Huddleston decided long ago that she wasn't going to let that tramp ruin her life. She pretended she didn't know a thing about her husband's passion for Georgina and also pretended she was Georgina's friend. When a nosy friend tried to inform Mrs. Huddleston about it under the guise of concern for her, she used profanity out loud for the first time in her life. That friend never talked to her again.

But if I get out of the car now, he may kill someone, maybe a baby or a little child. She knew it wasn't right that he drove without being able to see the lights. Mrs. Huddleston had never been able to have a baby of her own, but she had a massive soft spot inside her that made her stop and coo over babies in buggies. She had even stooped so low as to beg perfect strangers to let her hold their babies just for a minute. In the old days, some mothers would let her. But it had been decades now since anyone let her place her old wrinkled face on their baby's cheek.

"I'm not afraid of cancer. I'm angry at how it's foisted on us," said Gina.

Standing close to Gina, Morrison felt so woozily happy that he had to concentrate to remember what *angry* meant.

"I love you with all my ventricles and from the bottom of my hammertoes," he whispered into her ear. "Let's have a baby."

This was not the first or second or third time Morrison had brought up having a baby. He had brought it up almost every day for the past year.

So far, she always answered the same way. "I have a baby."

And Morrison always said back, "I love your dog baby, but wouldn't it be great to have a real baby?" He had high hopes that one day Gina would say, *Hell yeah, let's get started on that real baby today.* He wasn't really in a rush. They had all the time in the world.

⁂

Mr. Huddleston had lost all feeling in his right foot. His gas pedal foot. He stomped down hard on the pedal, like he was stomping his foot on the pavement to get the blood circulating again. He stomped down again and again. Why couldn't he feel anything?

The car sped up like crazy. It went right through a stop sign on Chestnut Street, barely missing a woman bicycling with a toddler strapped into a plastic seat behind her. The woman shouted after him but Mr. Huddleston didn't hear a thing. He stomped down hard on the pedal again.

Mrs. Huddleston went to a place inside herself that she knew very well. It was a place where she could be entirely by herself, with all humiliation left outside. She pictured it like a tree house in deep woods. He couldn't rage at her or shame her while she was there. In fact, she didn't even know a man named James G. Huddleston when she was like this. She was in a kind of trance where she didn't hear sounds from the outside world, only the birds in the woods and the happy singing of a very little girl.

⁂

"What's that noise?" Gina said.

"I don't hear anything," Morrison said. He always said Gina could hear someone sneeze three blocks away. He was watching PrettyBoy and Sukie run in perfect unison in a crazy pattern, round and round the dog park. That's how he thought of Gina and himself, moving together through life bending and twisting as fate flung things at them, never leaving each other's sides until they were very old and watching their great-grandchildren play.

"Get PrettyBoy," Gina said. "Now."

She started running and screaming his name, but PrettyBoy was having the time of his life. He kept switching directions like Gina was a big dog he was playing with, zipping around in crazy circles. He even ran between Gina's legs a few times very fast, while she struggled to grab him.

"What? Why?" Morrison said.

Gina's eyes were fixed on the Cadillac aiming straight for the dog park. Morrison followed her eyes.

"Get him," she screamed.

Morrison heard the roaring now, like a monster truck at a rally. Then he saw the Cadillac barreling toward them, picking up speed. He screamed an unintelligible sound like in a bad dream where you want to yell *HELP* but you can't get your tongue lined up and your mouth in the right position because everything is happening so fast, and they were all sitting ducks trapped between the park fences. The dog people started screaming and running after their dogs and then. Time. Slowed. Down. As. The. Two. Ton. Car. Came. Right. Through. The. Dog. Park. Fence. Tearing. A. Big. Hole. In. It. And. Crushing. Sukie. Into. A. Ball. Of. Fur. And. Blood. Before. Crashing. Into. The. Irish. Memorial. And. Stopping.

When their car doors were pulled open, the Huddlestons spilled out onto the dog park lawn like children rolling down a hill. They had never warmed up to the idea of seat belts and had never buckled themselves in, for all the years they had owned the car.

Mrs. Huddleston looked up at the clouds through the bare tree branches above. She felt good, peaceful for a change. Nothing hurt. She didn't have any duties right now. No calling out *STOP* and *GO*. The ride was over. She was happy to be lying on her back on the ground like a baby on a picnic blanket. She smiled up at the faces.

Mr. Huddleston had landed flat on his back in a mud puddle. He felt the wet spot spreading across his backside and was enraged. How could he show up at Georgina's funeral with shit-like stains on his trousers?

"Is this New Jersey?" he shouted up to the faces leaning over him.

"FUCKING New Jersey's over there, you FUCKING asshole," one of the dog people shouted back to him. "Fuck is wrong with you, old man. You killed a dog, motherfucker. You know how many people you almost wiped out, you crazymotherfucker?"

Mr. Huddleston heard only a distant, troubling "fucking." He sighed and his frail body sunk a tad deeper into the mud.

❧

After the ambulance. After the police. After Gina and Morrison helped Sukie's people gather her remains for cremation. After walking Sukie's people to the vet and handing over the small still bundle wrapped in someone's jacket. After staggering home on shaky legs. After the incredible relief of entering their apartment full of their own wonderful smells, sinking onto their sofa, and opening a bottle of deep red wine. After Morrison called out sick from work. They sat. Not talking. At all. For a long time.

Feeling the blood return to their knees. Feeling the wine start to work on their shakes. Not talking. But holding on to each other and PrettyBoy and tears rolling down their faces thinking of Sukie and the old people splayed on the ground like dolls that a child had thrown down. Drinking. Sitting in stunned silence. Drinking. Staring at the sun coming in through the bare windows. Drinking. Laughing when PrettyBoy finally raised his head up from Gina's lap to stare fixedly into their eyes, and gave a quick lick first to Morrison's cheek and then Gina's. As if he was saying *Oh people, calm down, you're all right, nothing happened. You're safe. For now.*

The Last Time

WHEN YOU'RE a funeral driver you can never turn on the radio to hear the baseball score. Chew gum. Sneeze. Slurp coffee. We have to be silent. No comforting, no consoling. If we find a hand in our lap unzipping our pants, we are to chalk that up to the craziness of grief and not give in to it.

All these years, I only gave in one time. I believe that is a grievous sin that I'm still paying for. She was a single mother. I don't know if there ever was a dad or if it was one of those insemination deals where she picked a father from a book, bought his sperm online, and got pregnant in a doctor's office, lying there on a table all by herself.

They usually don't let family ride in the hearse with the coffins. But she raised such a stink they let her. So she was riding all alone in the hearse with two tiny caskets in the back. Twin babies who died from being born too young and wanted too fiercely. They were flame babies, hovered over and snuffed out like little candles.

You read the newspapers and see pictures of those refugee children run out of their countries by war—no shoes, no food, all bony ribs and big eyes, running for their lives to camps across the border.

I bet my bottom dollar some of them grow up strong and make it back to their homes, because they're tough. But it seems to me that these insemination babies are like hothouse orchids, look at them crosswise and they go limp. You wouldn't catch them being able to run shoeless into the next country on no food and water.

That strong stock we don't have here anymore, with all these fifty-year-old pregnant women and people taking all kinds of medicines for their bad moods or jumpiness or whatnot. We are weak and getting weaker. I say this as a weak man myself. I'm ashamed to say I drink.

Anyway this woman's grief was so large and her need was so great, it knocked me down. I found myself flat on my back with her mouth bringing me to attention, and then she mounted me like I was a pony that she paid for a ride on and she was going to get her money's worth. Later I wondered if she was ovulating and she thought I would be a free source. Maybe she wanted babies so bad she couldn't wait and it didn't matter who the man was, even a sorry specimen like me. The joke was on her. I don't have any sperm alive in me. I took care of that a long time ago. What comes out of me is dead already.

See, I think like that. I am full of dead sperm. I am a man who made my living from death. Seems to me death has been my fate in life. Take the black rat living in my house. I still see it plain as day, out of the corner of my eye. It's not real. It's the start of cataracts, the eye doctor tells me. But for so many years, right after I would see that black rat darting across my floor, the phone would ring and it would be my boss, the funeral director, telling me where to show up for the next funeral. My heart thumped with surprise every single time.

You'd think you would know when something big in your life is wrapping up, when it's the last time you'd do it. But that's not how life works. So I didn't know that this would be the last funeral for me, after fifty-two years.

I drove the biggest limousine that day. When I pulled up to the beat-up row house in the West Philadelphia neighborhood, in a block sandwiched between an abandoned warehouse and a scary neighborhood playground, its faded red door was standing wide open. One child came out, then another and another and another in what seemed to be an endless stream of children pouring out. I blinked my eyes.

The children stood in the sidewalk like statues, waiting. Finally a man came out, wearing one of those slings that held a tiny baby across his chest. The baby had a lot of straight black hair that moved all by itself in the breeze. The man had a blob of toothpaste on the corner of his mouth.

I opened all the doors of the limousine and gestured for the children and man to get in. I counted. There were seven boys and girls who climbed in. With the baby up front, there were eight children in my car that day and their mother in a coffin waiting at the church. I thought my heart would burst.

Why was I even driving that day? It was my day off but my boss, Jimmy, called me in. I never said no. I had nothing else to do until my 5 p.m. drinking time started. The other drivers were all younger men, in their forties and fifties. Jokers. Slapdash. Not the sharpest knives in the drawer. A thought buzzed around my ear like a fly I kept swatting away—that my boss sent me to this family for a reason but I didn't know why.

The car filled with the smell of unwashed children, a mixture of pee, fried food, and sour milk. Two of the little girls wore ballerina tutus over their pants. One of the boys wore one sneaker and one dress shoe and he was old enough to know better. His mother would not have let him out of the house like that, I couldn't help but think. She would have made him crawl under the bed until he found the other dress shoe. One of the older girls had helped herself to her mother's red lipstick. She looked so terribly wrong that I was dying to wipe it off, but I did nothing. The whole lot of them looked like a tribe of gypsy children, with raggedy hair and snotty noses.

The father sat in the seat next to me. He wasn't helping the kids put their seatbelts on or checking to make sure they all got in or anything. He stared out the front window. An old woman finally came out limping and settled herself next to him. She smelled of hairspray and sweaty underarms. Her eyes were vacant, nobody home.

Nobody told me there would be all these little children. They didn't have car seats and I knew we didn't have any back at the funeral home. Usually people brought their own car seats or they drove children in their own cars but not this time. That little baby was too newborn to be out in the world at all. Everything was wrong about this.

I pulled out slowly. He started to talk the minute we started moving. He wasn't talking to me or to his mother. His voice was directed straight up into the air.

"I swear to God," he said. "This is not on me and nobody better put it on me. No way am I taking the blame for this shit. She wanted a big family and she got one."

I heard the ragged voice of a man who hadn't eaten or slept in days, the crazy raised up from deep inside and spilling out his lips as if his children couldn't hear him. But they could.

"Who dies in childbirth in this day and age?" he said. "I told her we should stop but she said no. She made this happen all by herself. It's not my fault we had all these kids."

The older woman sighed and patted him on the leg. He flicked her off like she was a mosquito.

"I don't know who she thought she was. Some woman out of an old movie or something. We aren't even religious. It wasn't like some priest or the Pope told us to be fruitful and multiply. We have no goddamned excuse. She just wanted it. She kept going. She said she liked being pregnant. I think she liked the attention, that's what I think. She got the attention and I got the bills," he said.

"Dad," one of the kids said. "Dad. Dad. Dad. Dad."

He ignored the child.

"Why didn't I put my foot down?" he said. "I knew better. I knew this was a mistake. Just because you like doing something doesn't mean you get to do it over and over again, with no thought to the consequences."

The woman sighed again. Seemed like grief stole all her words and gave the man extra.

"Mommy. Mommy. Mommmmmmy," a child screamed.

"There is no Mommy. Mommy's gone," the man shouted. "I told you and told you."

The child wouldn't stop, screamed louder and louder. That made the rest of them start screaming and sobbing too. I never heard a cacophony like that in my whole life. And I never wanted a drink so much in my whole life. My hands itched with the need to hold a big glass full of whisky. My mouth watered at the thought of swallowing that peace and quiet down inside me, that holy warmth, my lifeblood. But I never traveled with whiskey stashed under the seat or in the glove compartment. I knew better than to tempt myself that way.

I stopped the car finally on Kelly Drive, the twisty road beside the Schuylkill River that led to the church and cemetery, pulling into an empty parking lot along the river. I wasn't going to say anything, just sit quietly with them until the noise died down or the adults spoke up sensibly.

But when he did speak up again, it didn't help.

"I should have pulled out," he said. He looked down at the baby in the sling across his heart and said, "What am I going to do with you?"

He turned around to the children and said, "You can scream all you want but Mommy is gone and she's not coming back. That's what she gets for being a stubborn bitch."

I slapped the dashboard. "Do something," I said to the older woman.

She sighed and held up her hands.

"Sir," I said to the man. "May I please speak to you privately? Will you step out?"

People should at least try to be strong at funerals. For their children's memories at least. He wasn't even trying. He was killing these children's chances of ever growing up with their souls intact. He was throwing them live into the pits of Hell with his words.

"No, I will not," said the man. "I don't have to speak to you. I am not speaking to you."

His eyes were glassy and unfocused. He looked so loosely wrapped in his skin that a slight touch might collapse him into a heap of bones and muscles and nerves.

I stepped out of the car then. I couldn't just sit there and do nothing. I had no plan but a vague thought that maybe if I shocked him by getting out of the car, he might hear himself and shut up. He might say, *Hey man, you have to get us to the funeral. Her children need to say goodbye to her.*

Instead, he moved over into my seat and turned the car on. Which he was able to do because I had left the keys in the ignition like the stupid oafish dolt that I am. There he was, a deranged man in a car full of his eight children and his senile mother, poised on the edge of a river.

That crazy man did it. He shifted into drive and stepped on the gas. The car roared forward straight toward the river, crashing past the flimsy barrier. I screamed loud enough to wake the dead, ran after the car, and lunged for the car handle. Mercifully the door opened. I threw my body into him and yanked the key out. The car finally stopped on the sloped river bed, its head bowed down inches from the water.

"Help me," he said, crying. "Somebody help me." The sounds he made were like someone being stabbed in every tender spot he had. The louder he wailed, the quieter the children got until all you could hear was the man's guts spilling out into the air over the river.

I shoved him over and climbed back into the limousine. For a long time, my hands would not stop shaking. Try as I might, I could not steady them to drive. My mobile phone vibrated in my shirt pocket.

I knew it was my boss calling to see what was keeping me. I pictured the cemetery with its open grave, the church next to it full of people waiting to see the family troop in, the father leading the way with the newborn across his chest like an offering, then the bigger children holding hands with the smaller children.

Finally, a long time later, my hands stopped shaking a bit and I backed up into the parking lot and pulled out onto the road. I drove on slowly, my warning lights flashing red so everyone knew to go around us. I was seeing the road through a massive gray haze in my brain, with my mind replaying the car plunging into the river over and over again. I don't know if the father was still talking or the children were still screaming and crying. I blocked everything out that would stop me from getting these people to the funeral. I was a horse with blinders on, clip-clopping like the dumb beast I am.

When I finally got there, my boss was red-faced and pacing. I opened the door and tried to get out but I fell to the ground in a heap and looked up at him.

"Jimmy," I said, "I'm done, man."

He thought I was drunk. That the day finally came when I brought my weakness to work with me. That I drove this huge, terrible family here with whiskey in me.

"I'm not drunk, Jimmy," I said. "You can test me."

"Shut up, Sam," he said. "Get up off the ground, man." He tried to pull me up but all the life had gone out of my legs.

"Leave me be," I said. "Please. Get them out of the car."

"I can't leave you here on the ground, for God's sake. Making a spectacle of yourself." Jimmy gestured to the other guys to pick me up.

It was the strangest feeling, being lifted up by my arms and legs and carried into the church. Like being a little baby again, other people in charge of moving you from here to there. It felt wonderful to be so helpless. It felt true, like what was happening on my outside finally matched my inside.

They laid me down in the last pew of the church.

"Do you want an ambulance?" one of them asked.

"No. Just let me lie here," I said. I wanted nothing more than to be left alone in my failing body, my heart still thumping like a wild thing.

The funeral progressed around me. Flat on my back, I couldn't see anything but I heard snatches of it, like a bad dream. A sneeze that sounded like a scream. A baby laughing, a shocking sound that landed like a grenade. A bagpipe playing "Amazing Grace" in the wrong tempo and with many false notes. A man telling a long story from the altar about his dog who died. *What?* I thought. *I must be hearing that wrong. No one would go on about their dog while a woman is lying dead in front of him.*

A woman tried to read a poem but she was stuck like a broken record. "Do not stand at my grave and cry; I am not there. I did not die. I did not die. I did not die. I did not die. I did not die. I did not die. I . . ." Finally she gave up and sat down.

A man slid into the end of my pew. He was very young and skeletally thin. His shoulder bones poked out of his shirt and it looked like it hurt him to sit on his bony bottom. He didn't look at me. Maybe he thought this was a new accommodation for the disabled, letting a man lie flat on his back in a church pew. Then I felt the pew begin to shake. He was crying silently, his whole body rocking, crashing into the back and then pitching forward.

I wanted to say out loud, *Don't worry, whatever you've done, it isn't as bad as what I did. I entered the body of a bereaved woman on her way to the burial of her babies. I drove a deranged man and his brood of innocent children to the brink of drowning in the river. I drank so many nights of my life away that no one can save me now.*

But I didn't say any of that. If a funeral man knows anything, it's that he is to be silent in the face of grief. Let others weep and wail. Let others release their terrible feelings outside of their bodies. A funeral man has a job to do, silently on the sidelines, arms folded across his chest, waiting for it all to unfold.

As I watched him leave a few minutes later, I thought maybe that young man was her doctor. The one who let her die in childbirth. The first death he ever had a part in, but not the last. Whoever he was, he wasn't crying for her. He was crying for himself, for what he now knew and couldn't wish away. That he held in his hands the means of his own destruction, like all of us. Like me. The whiskey, the keys, the zipper, my wounded heart skipping beats until it stops one day.

The organist played the last slow, sad song and I heard the thumping, rolling coffin cart coming down the aisle. It stopped near my pew. The man with his infant strapped to his chest stood and looked at me, still flat on my back like both my legs were broken. His eyes were more alert now. His hands rested on his baby's head and his children bumped around his legs.

"I'm sorry," he said. "Man, I messed up back there. Forgive me, all right?"

I raised my head and nodded yes, yes, yes and put my hand over my heart. It was pounding like a broken dam with water pouring over it.

I rose on shaky legs and followed the family and the mourners out of the church, passing right by the other funeral men like they were strangers in black suits and nothing to do with my life ever again, as separate from me as the cormorants flying over the river flapping their loony wings while I stumbled my way home.

Chew On That

THESE DAYS, Breena Chew raises rabbits. She'll tell you that first, before admitting to be a wife and mother and a native of Penny Pot, New Jersey. She used to be another kind of woman, who wore short-shorts and halter tops, who had a string of boyfriends stretching from Cape May to Philadelphia from age thirteen right up until she married Jack at twenty. Back then, Breena liked to go out dancing and loved her drug store cashier job. She had been thrilled to get off her dad's farm and move to a tiny apartment in dangerous, glamorous Atlantic City and run around with her girlfriends all night long.

Jack doesn't know where this rabbit-raising woman came from. Somewhere along the line, Breena gained seventy-five pounds and started building rabbit cages all over the backyard.

Raising rabbits was an urge that came over Breena, like the urge to get married. She doesn't know where the woman she used to be went either, but it doesn't bother her. She watches change in her life like it's happening to someone else. *Would you look at that? This is me now, a fat woman with eighty-three rabbits, proud owner of a stall at the South Jersey Farmers' Auction every Friday night.*

Breena looks like a good-time gal. The male farmers flock around her at the auction, drawn by her permanent grin, curvy body, floppy blonde ponytail, and strong arms as she unloads her truck and hoists her cages on the tables by herself.

"Those rabbit cages are cleaner than our house. Can't you do better than this? Aren't we as important as those rabbits?" Jack tries to make deals with Breena. "How about two cages? Or half the rabbits you have now?"

"That's my livestock, honey. You can't ask me to give up my livestock." No effing way is Breena making a deal like that.

What Jack really wants is to turn back the clock, freeze their life back ten years ago, Breena knows. That man has no sense of the flow and mystery of life. How life changes you, twists beneath you without warning, turns beloved into stranger. Life did quite a number on you, too, Jack. She hasn't seen the guy she married for quite some time.

Breena never asked Jack to give up any of his obsessions: the beer-making that took over their basement and kitchen for a solid year, the photography darkroom, the long-distance bicycling. Or the drinking, for that matter. He had been a happy drunk, laughing with his friends and then falling over asleep. He stopped finally because he didn't want to be a bad example to his sons, didn't want them to grow up with a drunk for a father. Bad enough they have a fat rabbit farmer for a mother. He didn't say that out loud, but Breena knew.

It would have been bad for Cal, their normal son. But their other boy, ten-year-old Dirk, wouldn't know if his father was a drunk or not. He's slow. Breena and Jack are supposed to call him a special needs child and refer to him as being on the autism spectrum. Before that, doctors and teachers called him severely developmentally delayed. Delayed to Breena means you're late for the bus but you'll catch the next one. *Dirk is so delayed that he doesn't even know what a bus is,* she thinks.

She's fed up with all the labels and acronyms that litter their life like junk mail—Pervasive Developmental Disorder-Not Otherwise

Specified (PDD-NOS); Individualized Educational Program (IEP); Facilitated Communication (FC); Behavioral Intervention Plan (BIP). *I'd like to BIP your IEP on the PDD-NOS something fierce.*

Breena calls Dirk slow and dares the doctors to say one word to her about it. The daughter of a South Jersey pig farmer, she was raised to respect nature's variations, not to carry on about a mistake nature makes. But Jack is a social worker and he's used to making everyone better. He doesn't accept Dirk's limitations. He's constantly bringing home books and articles, joining internet support groups, bothering Dirk's teachers. Not Breena. Not anymore.

She stopped reading and thinking about it all five years ago, after Jack brought home an article about the link between autism and vaccinations. Breena read about half of it, stories of how normal, happy, laughing, talking children turned autistic overnight when their neurological systems failed under the assault of vaccines, how parents were banding together to fight the schools' insistence on vaccinations. The article hit her like a sucker punch to the stomach. She threw it down in disgust.

"I can be Dirk's mother. I can take care of him the rest of my natural life. I can tolerate the endless meetings with teachers, the stinking paperwork, and the stupid programs they cook up for him. I can do everything and anything I have to do for him. But I am not taking the blame. The law makes us vaccinate our babies. The schools enforce it. The doctors schedule it. What was I supposed to do?"

Now their son, who had started out a golden-haired, smiling baby, babbling early, rolling over delightedly, crawling like a son-of-a-gun, is dull-eyed and very odd. He sits under tarps over wood piles in the yard, spends hours underneath the heavy blue plastic, staring down at the dirt. He screams without warning. He can't read or listen to someone read to him. He hasn't said a word in years. He is gone somewhere deep inside and no one can reach him. Breena refuses to feel bad, whether it was vaccinations, her anger at getting pregnant again so soon, her genes, tight jeans, or whatever else she supposedly did wrong.

Breena finds peace with her rabbits. They fascinate her, their small furriness a constant pleasure. To her amusement, she finds that she's just like her dad, who used to lean on his shovel at the end of every day, staring at his pigs with wonderment. She wishes Jack could find something to give him true and lasting pleasure.

She tried ducks before rabbits, but it was a disaster. The Chews live on the edge of the Pine Barrens, a vast wild forest preserve, and raccoons are a problem. Raccoons used to come after the ducks at night, pull their little legs right off their bodies through the cage openings. The cries were terrible. Breena had to stitch up the ducks. Most of them lived fine with one leg but she couldn't take it. And no one wanted to buy one-legged ducks, that's for sure.

Breena sells a dozen rabbits a week for $8 each at the auction. Then she takes her money and buys bigger rabbits so her stock keeps improving. She'll sell a small one for $8 and buy a big one for $13. It's hard to pick a good breeder. Sometimes they look big and healthy, but their litters are born dead or deformed, for no reason. There's a lot to learn and a lot to do. They keep her very busy, the way she likes it.

In front of company, Jack likes to embarrass Breena by saying she's just like his Cousin Henry. That's a real funny story, at least the first thousand times you hear it. Cousin Henry was retarded. He loved to sell things. That's about all he could do. So every week he fetched a bag of soft pretzels, the kind Philadelphia is famous for. He bought them for a dime each and sold them up and down the South Philadelphia streets for a nickel each.

"Breena is another Cousin Henry," Jack said. "He just loved to sell those pretzels. And people loved to buy them for a nickel."

Every Friday night, when Breena comes home from the auction, he gets going on her like that. He asks how many rabbits she sold, then how many she bought. She tells him the truth, beyond caring what he thinks. She knows the numbers don't add up.

She overhears Jack talking on the phone to one of his friends, saying her rabbits are causing trouble in their marriage. Being raised in the city, he's at a disadvantage here. All he can see is the trouble and time that raising animals takes, but the challenge and peacefulness is hard for him to see. It takes a long time before you make a profit in animals, Breena will give him that. You can't calculate it on an hourly rate like being a secretary or hairdresser or some of the other jobs she could get out there in the world.

Jack tries to convince Breena that a real world job would be better for her, that she's wasting her time on rabbits.

Time. She has all the time in the world, that's the truth. Cal is into sports now, almost a teenager. So he stays after school to play whatever sport he's in that season, then he takes the latest bus so he doesn't get home till dark. Dirk gets out at 2 p.m. every afternoon and the special bus lets him out at their driveway soon after.

Back when Breena was in school, the kids used to call it the "retard bus" but kids are nicer about name-calling now. That bus is full of kids these days. There's a diagnosis every minute at that school, an epidemic of autism and learning disabilities.

After he shoots off the bus like a human cannonball, Dirk crawls under the tarp and stays there until his father gets home and drags him out.

"Why do you let him sit under there? He should be practicing his skills. You should keep him active."

Breena hates it when Jack takes that instructive tone with her. Like she knows nothing and he knows everything.

She knows some things, all right. She knows it's better for Dirk to sit under his tarp with her peeking under it every so often, smiling at him, than to be poking and prodding him to perform like everyone else in his life. She's happier, he's happier. She has hours every day to sort out her rabbits by size and breeding capability, clean their cages, give them fresh food and water, plan her next auction trip, and fill out their hutch cards and breeding records.

"I'm busy," Breena warns. Don't push it, don't push me.

"Busy in bunny town," he mutters, shaking his head. "While my son sits under a piece of plastic, watching dirt."

Breena would rather have a knock-down, drag-out than this under-the-breath nastiness. She'd rather have him look her in the eye and tell her they are in trouble than hear it behind the kitchen door.

He stalks away. Breena opens the door to her favorite cage, the one holding her newest and most beautiful Angora does. Rabbits are amazing, how fast they grow, how many kinds there are. People who don't know any better think a rabbit is a rabbit, but there are so many varieties, all different and special in their own way—Palamino, Siamese Satin, Champagne d'Argent, Chinchilla.

Breena brushes them and holds them, gives them funny names like Mr. Hopitola and Ms. Fluffaruma. People think they are dumb animals, but rabbits have feelings. Breena knows them to be as moody as humans, lethargic and snappy when the weather is rainy and gray and perking right up when it's a warm, sunshiny day. They can scream too. Sound just like you and me.

Breena's sister Marlene, married four times, says, "The very thing you fall in love with is the thing you despise in the end. I finally learned that lesson."

Breena never knew what Marlene meant before, but she's starting to get a glimmering. What she had loved about Jack was his optimism, his hunger to do good in the world. But where does that get them right now? He bangs his head against a brick wall every day and it's getting to where she can't stand to see it anymore. The rabbits are not their trouble. Not by a long shot.

Jack wants Dirk to go on a special diet he read about that's supposed to be miraculous for kids like him. Breena listens, reads the instructions, and turns it over in her mind. It's about the tenth time they've tried a diet like this, with no additives, no dairy, no gluten, no preservatives, and mostly raw food. Some doctor in New York City is having astounding success with it. Four parents on a website raved about it, so Jack's all excited about its potential. The problem is that Dirk only likes fried bologna, string cheese, and Pop-Tarts.

Breena ponders the diet. Was she supposed to starve the kid by taking his beloved foods away and replacing them with cold, hard, uncooked things in colors he didn't trust? She knew how much she'd hate it if someone took her Little Debbie snack cakes away. Little Debbie and she had a standing date, every night after dinner. It's not that she is lazy. If she thought it'd do any good, she'd make a mountain of brown rice, peel a bushel of carrots every day.

She chooses to be a good sport to please Jack, indulge his fantasy of a cure for Dirk. So Dirk's dinner tonight is attractively arranged cherry tomatoes, celery sticks filled with organic peanut butter, and apple slices.

"What the fuck," Dirk blurts out, as clear as a bell. He's not looking at his plate or touching his food. He stares at a cobweb high above him.

"Bro," Cal laughs. "Where'd you hear that, little bro?"

"Don't encourage him by laughing," Jack says. "You're his big brother. You have to help him. And call him by his name."

"Come on, Dad," Cal is unruffled. "He doesn't talk for five years and then he says 'What the fuck'?"

Jack takes Dirk's chin in his hand. "Don't say that. Say something else, anything else."

But Dirk is silent.

Breena has an idea. When she's alone with Dirk, she teaches him to say, "What the frig?" She waits till she hears him mutter the other phrase, then she repeats it with *frig* instead. He's a little poet, likes the sound of *fuck*. It is a good, strong word that feels great in the mouth. But just for fun, now that he has the hang of talking, maybe he'll try out the sound of *frig* too. It works.

"What the frig?" Dirk says at dinner the next night.

Breena and Cal can't stop laughing. Cal is laughing so hard he spits milk out.

"What the frig, Dirk," Breena repeats enthusiastically.

To Jack, who is shaking his head, Breena says, "That's better, isn't it?" If only he could be happy for small victories. But he slaps his palm down hard on the table and leaves.

❧

It comforts Breena to take care of little things. She walks to the middle of the hutches and disappears from the view of the house, surrounded. It's a city of cages, row after row laid out like streets in her backyard. It's her city and she's the mayor.

When she strolls down the rows, her rabbits rustle and hop excitedly. As mayor-god, she decides who goes to auction, who breeds, who stays and who goes. Hours go by so fast back here. Days, too. Breena is so sure of herself in this city. She's powerful and smart here. It's a drug she gives herself, an instant high and a resting place.

Back inside, she weighs Dirk, noticing his ribs poking out more than usual after a week on the raw food diet. He has lost five pounds, shivers in the cold bathroom. She pours her large body around him, holds him the way he likes, from behind so he can't see her face.

"No more diets," she announces at dinner, placing a plate of fried bologna and Pop-Tarts in front of Dirk.

"I'll quit my job and take over with him," Jack threatens.

Breena ignores him. She sees he is itching for a fight. She doesn't want to argue in front of Cal. Jack doesn't mean it anyway.

"Don't try to help him, then. Is that your brilliant solution?" Jack says. His eyes roll wildly around the room, like he's looking for an answer written on the walls.

"He's lost five pounds. This is not the answer," Breena answers.

Jack picks up his plate, goes to the kitchen to eat.

"Is Dirk ever going to get better?" Cal asks.

"No. Probably not," Breena says.

Cal nods gravely. He's going to take after her. She's proud of him. The religion in this family is acceptance and realism. See, once you accept, you can enjoy again. You can find something else to focus on. You can move along. She has to find a way to convince Jack, that's all.

Her sister Marlene sits on the back steps with Breena. It's a gorgeous afternoon and the smell of the scrub pines washes over them when the breeze blows their way.

"If I had to do it over again, I would have kept Number Two husband. Worked on it more." Marlene eyes Breena's body, gently asks, "Why don't you try something new? Counseling, a diet. Maybe take a class."

Admitting their troubles out loud to Marlene lowers Breena to despair. *I've started rolling down a hill and I don't know how to stop myself. I want to stop. Holding steady is what I need to do. Like a wild rabbit in the grass, hiding, waiting.*

Dirk is saying more words these days. Filthy words, but words nonetheless. *Blowjob* floats out clear as a bell, like a fart in church. *Asshole. Dickhead.* Thank God Jack hasn't heard him. Breena goes to school to see what is going on over there. Some new kind of speech therapy?

His teacher, one of those beaming do-gooders that you want to smash with something disgusting to see if that idiotic expression ever goes away, squirms in her seat when Breena begins.

"Dirk is saying some unusual words at home these days."

The teacher sighs. "Oh dear. Not Dirk, too. It's the new boy in his class." She whispers even though they are alone, "Tourette's Syndrome." Her breath is foul and Breena slides backwards in her seat to escape the fumes.

Breena has heard of that syndrome. It makes people shout obscenities. A lawyer in court yells *cocksucker* in front of the judge, jury, and witnesses. A sweet old lady shouts *muthafucka* in the grocery store. One of those illnesses that seems made up by the *National Enquirer*, too outlandish to be real, like "Baby Born With His Own Twin Inside Him."

Breena fights the urge to whisper back. "Is there anything that can be done about it?" she asks.

"His mother doesn't always give the boy his medication," the teacher says. "She claims it takes away his soul. Can you imagine?"

"Some people," Breena says. "Well, I just wanted you to know. It's a bit of a problem."

"I'm thrilled to pieces he's talking. Isn't it wonderful! You must be ecstatic."

"Wonderful," Breena replies. "Tickled to death."

The teacher wouldn't know sarcasm if it bit her in the foot. Or maybe she does and chooses to ignore it.

❧

At home, they are very polite to each other these days.

"Excuse me," Jack says as he squeezes by Breena in the hall.

A formal little family in a still little house. They are careful to talk about Cal's baseball team, the weather, the mean bus driver, what time they are having dinner.

Even Cal catches it. "Thank you for washing my uniform, Mom." "Dinner was very good, Mom." He has taken to watching his parents, following their moves with his eyes. "Can I help you out back, Mom?" Hearing his rough boy-into-man voice talk so sweetly to her almost breaks Breena down.

⁂

Marlene calls late at night, Breena sitting out on the back step watching the stars. Marlene is trying to make sense of her own life, the four men who came and went. Nothing Marlene says helps Breena but it is so good to hear a voice in her ear that she keeps listening.

"You get real close to each other right at the end," Marlene says. "You cry and clutch each other and say why, why can't we fix this? You look at each other and everything you feel and want is right there in your eyes and for once you both see it, in each other. And you think, oh *that's* what he couldn't say all those months. It gets real clear. But it's too damn late and you both know it. You're looking back on it all by then."

Marlene holds tears back, words choking in her throat. "It's so terrible, Breena. I wish I could save you from going through it. Protect yourself. It's so, so terrible."

"I'll be all right, Sis," Breena says and she means it. But at the same time, she's so frozen inside that her words sound meaningless, like she's speaking Portuguese to herself in a bad dream.

Jack is tiptoeing away from Breena, an inch at a time. She thought it was best to let him be, but now she is slapped by waves of rage and fear. She wants to snap him like a twig, stomp him like a yard beetle, for the pain of him turning his back on her. She feels them teetering on the edge of the biggest cliff of all. They are both throwing sticks down there, testing how far it is, how deep. Everything in her is pleading for them to turn back before it's too late.

⁂

The school wants Dirk to sing a song in a class performance. They have a notion that he can sing better than he can talk. They teach him "How Much is that Doggie in the Window." They play it over and over again, give Breena a CD for home, and ask the family to rehearse with him. Amazingly, he sings it in school after two weeks of this. How this will be transformed into a useful life skill, Breena couldn't claim to know, but they all seem tickled. Especially Jack.

The afternoon of the performance, Jack takes off work to attend. Breena can just hear him saying proudly, "My son is singing in a class play." He hums the song incessantly, sings it to Dirk as his bedtime song. *You are cruising for a bruising*, Breena thinks, but she doesn't burst his bubble.

They sit in the small auditorium and watch Dirk file onstage with his classmates. It's strange to see the motley crew that he spends his days with. Physical and mental disabilities all lumped together, so kids in wheelchairs with all kinds of tubes in their bodies are next to deaf and blind children, flanked by kids who look normal but who do wild things without warning like flapping their arms or making horrible grunting noises.

The Chews cannot pretend that Dirk doesn't belong with the special children. His mouth hangs open slightly and his eyes are unfocused, staring off into the ceiling. But he senses their presence. He runs off the stage, climbs down the steps on the side, and flings himself onto Breena's lap. His teacher follows, patiently takes his hand, and explains it's time to sing his song now.

Dirk screams as though red-hot knives are slicing off his fingers one by one. He will not calm down. The strongest male aide picks him up and deposits him gently in an adjoining classroom, sitting by his side. During tantrums, parents are supposed to stay away, let the child calm himself down. But Dirk's screams intensify and although it seems impossible they can get louder, they do.

The teachers try to begin the performance, one of them forcefully playing the piano. Breena wants to see what these kids can do, especially the ones who appear to be so incapacitated. She wants to be dazzled by their hidden talents. But the children refuse to sing. They are nervous, craning their heads around, staring at each other and at the door where Dirk's screams escape.

"I'll take him home," Breena says to the audience and teachers, getting up. "Then you can have your play." She's not going to sit here like a dope, hearing her kid scream like he's being murdered.

Jack gets up too, shuffling behind her. "What happened? What went wrong?" he mumbles.

"It was a dumb idea," Breena says, not caring if the teachers hear her. "Too much pressure on him. Why can't everyone leave him alone?"

Dirk shuts up immediately when they enter, gets up wearily and walks next to them to the car, and falls asleep on the way home. He's a beautiful curly-haired boy, blue eyes framed in long eyelashes, pink cheeks, perfect Cupid-bow lips. When his eyes are closed, it's hard to tell he's different from other children. Breena doesn't let herself fantasize like this very often, imagining him waking up and talking to her, "Mom, can I name the next litter? Can I go over to Timmy's to play?" Pointless. There's nothing more pathetic than a person who refuses to accept reality. Jack disgusts her right now, with his smashed-down face and sad eyes. It's incomprehensible to her that he is the same man she married. He's more like a morose cousin of the Jack she started out with.

"Who wants ice cream?" she pulls over at Big Eddie's roadside stand, with its giant statue of Big Eddie waving with a cone in his hand. She plows into a hot fudge sundae, loving its sweetness and dark warmth, sucking that sugar deep down into her. *Ahhhhh*. She ignores Jack glaring at her from the car.

❦

Breena keeps Dirk home from school for a week after that. She wants the incident to be good and gone from his mind, from everyone's mind. She feeds him only what he likes, fried bologna three meals a day and all the string cheese and Pop-Tarts he can stomach. She lets him sit under the tarp as much as he wants to.

"What did you guys do today?" Jack asks hopefully.

Breena guesses she's supposed to be teaching him to write a sonnet or to stand on his head.

"Mr. Hopitola and Ms. Fluffaruma had a litter today. Ms. Fluff made a very nice fur-lined nest, ripped the fur right off her own body and everything."

"When do you plan to take Dirk back to school?" Jack says.

When do you plan to touch me again? "When the cows come home. When pigs fly. When the fat lady sings," she spits out. She can read between the lines, knows him well enough to know what he's thinking. He trusts those moronic teachers more than her. Mr. Know-It-All. Mr. Superior.

"Start singing then," Jack says. "This has gone on long enough."

Breena gets up quietly and goes out to her hutches, walking down the rows in the early evening dusk, loving the smell of the rabbits, their flurry of interest in her. It's so still out there that she can hear the rabbits breathe and make snuffly sounds and squeaks.

Cal materializes next to her. "Hi, Mommy. How is everyone doing out here. How are the new babies?"

He means how are you feeling? A twelve-year-old boy who cares to see if she's hurting. She did all right with him at least.

She had been feeling detached, armored, but Cal melts her. Her eyes well up with tears and she's back in her body, feeling the solidness of her trunk. *There is so much of me wrapped around my heart. I am immense and tender.*

"What's that?" Cal jumps away from her, pointing toward a cage holding one of the new litters.

A two-week-old baby rabbit is stuck in the thick metal opening, his head poked through, cage wire twisted so tightly around his neck that it seems impossible he can ever be freed. His eyes bulge and his tiny body flails helplessly.

"Get wirecutters. Quick. In the shed. Hanging up."

Cal runs, reappears panting with the tool. It's too tight, there's no space between the bunny's neck and the wire. Breena edges the wirecutters in, trying for an angle that won't suffocate the bunny, cut off his air instantly, or impale him on a sprung metal end. She has one shot, but she needs to squeeze hard enough to release him on the first try or she'll kill him. She's not sure if she has enough strength in her hand.

"Get Daddy," she orders Cal, who runs into the house, leaping over food barrels and wood piles like a hurdler.

She's still working on an angle of insertion, trying to ignore the choking sounds coming from the bunny. She could kill him so easily.

Jack takes a quick look, grabs the wirecutters, hesitates for a second, then aims and squeezes in one motion, freeing the baby who falls to the floor of the cage. Breena opens the door and reaches in, feeling the bunny's breathing, the chest rising and falling in rapid pants, touching the fur around the neck for blood or broken bones.

"He's okay. He's going to be okay." She can't help it, she's crying with relief.

Jack holds Cal and her in a huge, tight hug and they rock together outside the cage until Cal breaks loose.

"Way to go, Dad. You the man. Excellent moves," Cal crows, jumping around them.

"At least I'm good for something," Jack deflates, pushing away from them. "Even if what I think counts for zero." He walks slowly back to the house.

"What's wrong? Did I say something bad?" Cal asks.

"It's nothing to do with you, Cal," Breena answers. She knows why stock parent phrases were invented, for times when there is so much to say, so little that would make sense. "Would you please go finish your homework now, Son?"

Cal stares at her for a long minute, then goes.

She stays for a long time with the bunny until he seems to be moving around okay. Then she busies herself filling water bottles and checking on does getting ready for their litters to be born, which usually happens at night.

Hard to believe that baby rabbits born tonight will be all grown up and ready to mate in six months, but it's true. Birth, mating, death —all happen with dizzying speed with rabbits and she notes it all in her records. Which doe mates with which buck, how many babies are born in each litter, how many are born dead, which ones survive their first days. Things happen in the rabbit world and nobody blames anyone else, nobody rages and turns on the other.

She tires herself out working late and falls asleep on the couch in her clothes.

❧

When Jack gets out of bed and goes to work, she climbs into their bed. It smells like him and their nights before this time. She stuffs the sheet into her mouth and remembers sex, the wild urgency and the whiff of their deepest selves that hung around afterwards. She waits for the world to stop shaking around her. What is happening is too huge to cry about. He's still here, she tells herself. Nothing has changed. It's just a hard time. But she cannot explain why her chest feels like a knife has been plunged deep inside. The pain is immense, holds her immobile in bed for hours.

❧

"I cannot bear this anymore." Jack's arm sweeps out to include Breena, the messy kitchen, the yard filled with rows of rabbit cages. "I don't want this. Any of this. I live in Rabbit Land. With a brain-dead son."

She sits quietly, listening. She had hoped that Jack would come home in a different mood, that last night was a bad poison that he expelled. Breena feels like she's guiding a raft through rapids. Here it comes. Hang on. She practices breathing steadily. What a miracle the body is, keeps right on going in spite of boulders flung at it, lightning crashing around it, avalanches of pain coming down. Thump, thump, thump—that heart beats harder but doesn't stop.

"Don't you have anything to say?" Jack asks.

"I am sorry for you if that's how you feel." Breena thinks they are bad breeders to have come to this sad state. They should be sold at auction for stew meat. The thought makes her smile inside, a little spark of hope. *I will be all right. We will be all right. Without you.*

"He is not brain-dead," she adds.

As if on cue, Dirk stands in the kitchen doorway. His beautiful face is expressionless, his eyes stare out the window, his blonde hair messy from sleep.

He sings in a high, pure voice. "How much is that doggie in the window?" And he won't stop, stands there and sings that dang song over and over, stumbling over the same words each time, but getting the melody exactly right.

Breena is laughing and crying at the same time, *boo-hoo-hoo-ha-ha-ha*. It's such a strange feeling, like having an orgasm while giving birth. Pain and pleasure jousting for the upper hand.

Jack is doing it too, *boo-hoo-ha-ha-ha*. For an instant, they are right there together, for the first time in a long time, facing their son and listening to his song. It's that closeness that Marlene tried to explain. No other two people could have this moment. They created this boy and this marriage and they are sitting there watching it die.

"I want to stop this. Can we please just freeze? Just wait. Don't say anything. Don't do anything. Please." Breena's words tumble out.

"I can't. I've had enough," Jack says. He is crying and won't look her in the eyes. "You have to accept reality. We have to move on. Separately." His voice sounds like heavy dirt, like shovels heaving up wet loads from the bottom of his stomach.

"Reality," Breena repeats. "Accept reality." She starts to roar now. It's unbearable that at the final moment, the word leveled against her is *reality*. She picks up anything in her path—eggs, dishcloths, cookbooks, coffee can, chairs—and tosses them, raging like a tornado trapped in a room. She's not trying to hit Jack or scare Dirk, but she does both.

Jack stands helpless, dishtowel draped over his head, egg dripping down his shirt. Dirk cowers in the doorway. Cal stands, shoulders squared, behind him.

Breena has to say something to her children. She repeats out loud what she hears rolling around in her head. "Relax. The worst is over."

It is not true. Every day she will think this is the worst, this has to be the worst. It takes a long time to smash a big woman down.

You Are the Bad Smell

"THIS ISN'T the one," she said, laying her hand on my arm. As if she was really sorry.

"Stick a fork in me. I'm done," I said.

"No. You're just upset. You thought this was the one."

"I can't do this anymore."

"It's only one house. Maybe the next one."

"It's seventy-three houses," I said.

"But we've come so far. You can't stop now. Absolutely not."

I thought if I banged her head against the concrete steps, her skull would not break. That's how hard she was. No one could win against her. Certainly not me. Certainly not her partner, who stood quietly in the corner, eyes cast upward.

The houses they did not buy: the contemporary with too much sunlight, the Dutch Colonial with a garage that was too small, the totally renovated rancher with an ugly view, the three-story Victorian with too much carpeting, the lakeside condo with not enough kitchen, the octagon house with too much personality, and the corner property with too many trees were some of the houses they did not buy.

Seventy-three houses they did not buy. Seventy-three houses I showed them and I knew this game. I knew how to play this game. But she was winning.

"I quit," I said.

She laughed. "We'll take a few days off."

I just won't return her calls, I thought. "Great idea," I said.

To her partner, I whispered, "I'm so sorry for you."

I could see that made the partner mad. But she was the long-suffering type, even with me.

"Not at all," her partner said. She held her head up high.

They were so beautiful, these two. Concrete Skull was a tall and crispy blond, with a gorgeous, wide smile and sharp, blue miss-nothing eyes. Long Suffering was short and olive-skinned, with a full bottom lip and a way of standing that showed off her large breasts. Her eyes were as patient as an animal watching for its turn at the watering hole.

I liked lesbians, made a specialty of selling houses to lesbian couples. There were tons of resales on those couples. A lot of them broke up after four or five years and then they put their houses back on the market and bought new ones with other women. I especially liked couples like this one, with their matching black Mercedes, big bank accounts, and high-salaried corporate jobs.

I liked lesbians, but I hated these two. They were realtor cock-teasers. Okay, I am a woman too and do not have a cock to tease, but you take my point. They showed you what they had, stroked you until you were so ready you could scream, then pulled back with a perfectly good reason that was totally bogus because the real reason they did not buy any of the seventy-three houses I showed them was because they were sizing each other up.

It had nothing to do with me. They were watching each other, waiting for the house that made one of them pant and scream. Then one of them would have the upper hand. The one who wanted it the most was the one who would have to grovel for as long as they lived in that house.

I know power struggles. I can smell them in the air after twenty-three years in the business and four marriages of my own. The smell is unmistakable, like a rotting carcass by the side of a road.

"The truth is I don't think there's anything special enough for you two on the market these days," I said. "I know you are busy women with highly responsible jobs and I feel just terrible wasting your time like this. We'll have to wait it out. Maybe in a few months, the market will improve. You two deserve something spectacular."

Concrete Skull didn't even show the flicker of interest that a cat has watching a chipmunk run by. Her blue eyes were steady beams.

"Next week," she said. "Set it up."

Long Suffering walked out to the Mercedes and leaned against it, staring intently into her mobile phone. She licked her lips slowly.

Concrete Skull whispered, "The truth is, I don't know if I should be buying a house with her. Look at her. She looks incredibly sexy, doesn't she? But she isn't."

"Why are you telling me this?"

"I feel so close to you. You feel like a friend after spending all this time with me." She beamed her big smile my way and it was like the sun coming out on my face. Okay, I am straight but I was not immune to her.

"If you're that unsure, you should wait before you look at houses."

"I operate on instinct. My gut tells me to keep looking. The right house will grab me. The house will say, come on in, you two. She'll relax in this bedroom. She'll attack me in this living room."

"That's crazy," I said.

"Why?"

"A house doesn't fix anything. Definitely not a sex problem."

"Who says? Maybe a house could fix something. Maybe no one lets it." She reached out and put both her hands over my hand. Her hands were warm. "Help me."

"For a smart woman, you're stupid," I said.

I thought if I insulted her, she'd go away and leave me alone. But she laughed.

"You're a cockteaser," I said.

"So I've been told. By better women than you." Her smile stayed fixed on her face, but she let go of me.

Good, I thought. *I'm finally getting to her.*

"So next week, then. Set it up for Saturday," she said.

Instead, I volunteered to work at an open house on Saturday. I was top agent in my office. I didn't have to work things like this. It was a sad, tiny little house with a persistent moldy smell. The owners were old. They didn't want to spend any money fixing up something that they were selling.

So the window shades were stained and yellow, the kitchen faucets dripped, the closets were dark and crammed full of crap, and the one and only bathroom had cracked vinyl flooring and a hole in the wall. The neighborhood was going seriously downhill. There was a meth lab one block over. No one cut their grass regularly. Next door, someone had propped two stained mattresses against their house.

The best I could do was burn vanilla candles for the smell and insist that the owners leave so they wouldn't hover anxiously over people trooping through. I didn't care. I was happy to be there. Anywhere but trapped with Concrete Skull and her little gal pal.

Only one couple ventured in during the first hour. I put on my honest, earnest face.

"It needs work, I won't lie to you. A little paint, new rugs. You can see for yourself. But this neighborhood is going through the roof in the next year. All signs point straight up for appreciation in value. If you bought this now and fixed it up a little, you'd have a hell of an investment."

The man had the hungry look. He didn't want to be poor all his life. His wife looked afraid. She didn't want to make a mistake.

I don't count what I said as lying because you never know. No one knows. The neighborhood could take an upturn. And a husband who wanders could stop, just like that. Sure. It could happen.

After they left, it was quiet for a long time. I turned up the volume on the smooth jazz CD, my music for selling shitty houses, and leaned back in my chair. I wondered who the lesbian couple was torturing this weekend, instead of me.

The door opened. They walked in. Long Suffering wouldn't look at me. Her eyes scanned the room like one of those searchlights that stores set up in their parking lots during closeout sales. Concrete Skull leaned in.

"We found you," she said.

"I thought we were taking a break."

"Break's over." Her voice was flinty, like the game we used to play when we were kids, hitting rocks with rocks to see what colors were inside.

"Don't you ever give up?"

"Never," she said. Her partner snorted.

Now, we'll get into it, I thought. *Come on, Long Suffering, make your move. Get in there. Speak up*. But she just turned, walked back to the car and got in, holding her elegant, round rump out on display for an extra second before it vanished into the Mercedes.

"Why me?" I asked. "Why don't you get a nice lesbian realtor? Maybe she'll do better for you. And she can come to your housewarming party, too."

"You know why I want you? Lesbian realtors think they don't have to work hard for me. Like just because I'm gay, I'll roll over and buy whatever they show me. Like it's about loyalty to the team instead of being about me and my money. Wrong. You're smarter than that. It's all about the deal."

I liked beating out lesbian realtors. I pictured them trotting out secret weapons with her—little lesbian in-jokes, little lesbian friends in common. And still I won. I admit I melted a little, flattered.

So we went on to the seventy-fourth house. It was a spectacularly ugly McMansion, huge, poorly designed and shoddily built, overpriced, on a barren lot on a busy street of a brand new development built over a landfill. But it was new, full of glitzy features like a master bathroom big enough to hold a party in and a temperature-controlled wine cellar in the basement, features that distract your eyes from the particle board walls and the cheap thin paint.

"Honey, this is it. This is the one," said Concrete Skull. She smiled her gorgeous beaming smile, charming as a kitten. It didn't sound convincing even to me. *This is a test. This is only a test. In the event of a real urge to buy a house, the voice is eager, excited, scared. So disregard this test. It is only a test.*

"No way," Long Suffering said. "I loathe the smell of this house. You've got to be kidding me. No freaking way."

"I was kidding. I hate it too," Concrete Skull said. "See, honey, we really are getting close. We both hate this one. So that's a good sign."

They both turned to me, waiting for my applause.

"Seventy-five," I said. "That's my limit. I warn you."

They both chuckled, like I was making a small, dumb joke.

I hate you both, I thought. *You are the bad smell.*

It was the seventy-ninth house where something changed. When we walked into the house, an elegant Colonial in the best neighborhood, fully updated and gorgeously decorated, I felt it. Somebody wanted this one, but I couldn't tell who. I felt like a squirrel on the curb, twitching at oncoming cars and deciding when to run. I studied one and then the other. Who was it?

I tried all my realtor tricks. I vanished into other rooms so they could talk privately. I acted nonchalant so they wouldn't feel pressure from me. I studied the seller's information sheet with just the right amount of scrutiny and indifference.

"It's quite old," Concrete Skull said finally. "It's an old house. They are asking a lot for such an old house."

Aha, I thought. *She wants it.*

"Honey, what do you think?" she asked. Her voice was a cat slinking along a high ledge. I didn't remember her asking that question in any of the seventy-eight previous houses.

"Oh, I don't know," Long Suffering said. She sounded bored but she was paying close attention, her brown eyes flickering madly. "Let's go on to the next."

I wanted to hit them with an ax and leave them bleeding to death on the Persian rug.

"I feel a very sexy vibe here," I said. "Classy, subtle, but very sexy. This is a house where you will have swank parties. I see gorgeous women in slinky dresses holding martini glasses."

"We met at a cocktail party just like that," said Concrete Skull.

"You pinned me to the wall," smirked her gal pal.

"After you practically pushed them in my mouth."

"You wanted me to."

"You wanted it worse."

I watched them like they were a nature channel show where all the animals are frolicking happily in the wilderness and you know there's trouble in the air, you are just waiting for the predator to pounce, for blood to be spilled. You know it will end badly and you can't tear yourself away.

"Let's write it up, girls. You can sign the agreement right now," I said. And they did.

When the radon test came back, Concrete Skull came to my office and cried. Her partner was on her way. We were supposed to wait for her, but Concrete Skull insisted on reading the report before she got there.

"We are the perfect couple," she cried, circling around the office, bumping into chairs and walls and cabinets, knocking over the waste basket.

"Everyone, everyone, everyone says so. But we can't do this one simple thing. I've done it with other women. It's no big deal. Go look at a few houses and buy one. What is happening? Why is this happening to me? I can't stand it. I'm being punished."

"It's only radon. Easily remediated," I said. "Punished for what?"

"I stole her from another woman. They have a baby. I'm mean to my mother. I hate my father. I've cheated on every woman I've ever been with. Is that enough?" She was really wailing now, working herself up.

"It's only radon," I said. I was enjoying myself immensely.

"I'm forty-one years old. I can't make any more mistakes."

"Everyone has some radon around here. This house is just a tad over the limit," I said.

"You don't understand. I am not everyone. I can't have it."

"Put a vent in the basement and we're good to go," I said.

"It's poison gas in the basement of our house. We'll be poisoned from below. What chance do we have to make it? Do you have any idea how many failed relationships I've had? This is my last chance. I'm not wasting it on her."

"It's not that bad. You're getting all carried away." I thought of Husband Number Three. I thought he was my last chance too, but along came Four. There were an infinite number of husbands out there, I found. I could have kept it up my whole life. Hello Five. Hello Six. Hello Seven.

Long Suffering showed up. "Do you still want it?"

"No," Concrete Skull sobbed. "It's a poison house."

"We'll keep looking then," her partner said, shrugging.

"It's our last chance. We'll never find another house as good as this one. This was the one. And it's ruined."

"So we'll buy it and fix it."

You fool, I thought. *You don't see that there is no way to win with her. The house is nothing. The house is a quicksand bog full of small dead things.*

"I'm sick of this," Concrete Skull cried. "I'm done."

"You're done. With looking?" Long Suffering stood in the doorway, legs planted wide. Slowly her face began to change. "With me? In front of her?"

"Just ignore me," I said. "Do what you have to do." You couldn't have pried me out of there with a crowbar.

I waited for Long Suffering to scream, curse, throw things. But she stood there silently for the longest time. And then she crumpled to the floor, making this odd squeezy sound, like a sharp beak was tearing at her lungs. She lay flat out, on her stomach, her arms around the base of my filing cabinet, and she kept making the squeezy sound. It was the most terrible sight I'd ever seen in my life. It was like watching somebody die.

I got down on the floor beside her, first sitting, then lying flat on my belly next to her. I felt my tenderest organs protected by the plush rug under me, then deeper to the wood floor and the concrete underpinnings. I was safe there. I rubbed her back. I patted her hair. I whispered in her ear, "You're okay. You will be. You're not going to die." It didn't help at all. Nothing does. Her back stayed stiff and the wrenching unbearable noise continued as Concrete Skull stepped over us both and left.

We waited, breathing in little tiny puffs, to see if she would circle back. We waited a long time until we felt the currents in the air settle down to normal rhythms and heard the birds outside in the trees begin to sing.

Dip Me in Honey and Throw Me to the Lesbians

WHEN SHE saw the baby, Jane was a little drunk from martinis at the art museum. Big martinis. Little baby. But not drunk enough that she imagined the little bearded baby, a girl in striped leggings and a raspberry dress, with curly blond hair on her head and on her face. Downy hair on her plump cheeks and tufts on her little chin. A hairy, little beard on a little baby girl. The baby's parents, a cool urban couple, were eating—the father holding her football style dangling over his forearm; the mother keeping one eye on the baby, as mothers do, while leaning in the opposite direction to talk and laugh with her friends.

The baby was inches away from Jane's elbow so she couldn't say anything out loud to her friends. She turned around to send eye signals to Leanna, but Leanna was fixated on the dessert case full of cakes. They and five other friends were in line at a tiny art museum area restaurant fashioned out of a hundred-year-old row house.

People were eating all around them in what would have been the house's entryway and living room. The kitchen was off the back. There was a twisty staircase with sloping, worn-out hardwood steps leading to another small dining room upstairs. It was the kind of place where you literally stood in the aisle next to the tiny tables of the restaurant looking down on other people's food. Those eating tried to ignore those standing and staring.

They had been standing there waiting for a long time even though they had a reservation. It was 10 p.m. They were starving. The hostess, who was usually stationed behind the dessert case by the door, had disappeared upstairs. She couldn't face them anymore. She had run out of excuses, having used up, "They're clearing your table right now," "Just a few more minutes, I promise," and all the other usual delaying tactics.

Jane and her friends hadn't eaten appetizers at the art museum event because they were saving themselves for this place afterwards. This cool little fabulous restaurant, the top-rated one in a neighborhood full of cool little fabulous restaurants. They were foodie and winey lesbians; that was their thing. They went from restaurant to restaurant, tasting and comparing, and they roamed the city going to happy hours, benefit fundraisers, and museum nights.

They were allegedly looking for other women but Jane thought the truth was they were all really happy being in a girl gang again. All of them had stopped using internet dating sites once they found this group. She noticed that they didn't reach out to each other for dates either. And as far as she knew, none of them were sleeping together. Without talking about it, they all knew what that would lead to eventually—an end to their happy social group and a return to empty weekends and no one to eat and drink with.

"If I pass out from hunger, I'm going to land right in that guy's osso bucco," Leanna said into Jane's hair. She moaned, "It smells soooooo good in here."

Jane took a chance and whispered back at Leanna, twisting her head around to get closer, "There's a bearded baby. Right there. Look."

"What's that?" said Leanna.

Jane mouthed, "A bearded baby."

"I don't know what that is," said Leanna. "Is that Australian slang for something delicious?" Jane had lived in Australia for a few years with her second ex and sometimes she'd break into Aussie talk. Leanna teased her about it regularly.

"No, it's an actual bearded baby. A baby with a beard," said Jane, trying to keep her voice very low.

"Not another name for a little tart? It sounds like a scrumptious little tart. Would you like a bearded baby? Take two, they're small," laughed Leanna.

Jane thought, *Man, she turns into a dimwit the minute she starts drinking martinis. Pay attention, Leanna. I'm trying to tell you something.*

Jane tried again. "Leanna, look. Red-haired couple with the blond baby."

Leanna searched through the diners. "Oh MY," said Leanna when she saw them.

The mother felt the two women looking at her baby. *You can feel eyes looking at you*, she thought, *it's true*. She was mightily sick of it. She wanted one night out with her friends, crunched together at a great restaurant over many bottles of wine. She wanted to walk home a little drunk with her husband and their baby and stumble happily into their house without anything making her mad. She wanted to be a regular mom with a regular baby. She felt like they were a celebrity family, the object of snuck glances, people mouthing things and rolling their eyes, whispering. Every time they went out in public, she felt like standing up and making a little speech—

My baby daughter has a beard. It happens. Every so often in nature, a baby is born with a beard. Some babies have birthmarks. Some babies have tongues too big for their mouths. Some babies are born without earlobes. My baby has a beard. I am not going to take a razor to her precious face. I am not going to give her toxic medicine. I am not going to do one damn thing about it. I am going to have a happy baby girl grow up with a beard and see what happens when she gets older. Maybe it will fall off all by itself. Okay, everyone? Back to your dinner now. Thank you for your concern

—which is really intrusive and insensitive voyeurism, by the way—and leave us the fuck alone.

Her husband said she should do it. If it was such a strain for her to feel the looks landing on her, if it felt like blows hitting her, if it felt so awful to her, then she should just stand up and give them a little talking-to.

He used expressions like that, *a little talking-to*. Who the hell talks like that? He was such a pedantic asshole sometimes. He sounded like an eighty-year-old schoolmarm. She hated him so much for his laid-back nature. Jesus, he acted like having a bearded baby was no big deal. It was a big fucking deal. If she heard that story about his niece Jammy one more time, how Jammy was born with a fuzzy back like a little bear cub and how all the fuzzy brown hair just disappeared—no problem—when she turned a year old. She wanted to scream every time she heard it. A face is not a back, you asshole. They could put clothes on Jammy and presto, just like that, she wasn't a freak baby any more. What were they supposed to do, put a face veil on their baby, cover her beard like she was a little Muslim?

She remembered the night she met him, at a huge peace rally where people were chanting and banging on drums and the night air was full of angry speeches and insistent calls to action. And there he stood, grinning like a fool. She thought, *Boy, that guy is a happy man, even on the brink of a catastrophic, immoral war. I want to be with him. I'll pick up happiness from standing next to him. Anything bad that happens in our life together will go easier with a happy man like that.*

Now she couldn't stand him. She would give anything for a flash of anger from him once in a while, an acknowledgment that they had been dealt a terrible hand. *My baby has a beard and it's all your fault,* she thought. *Your genetic contribution made this happen. Not mine. My baby has flawless skin. Your baby was born with a fucking beard and it hasn't gone away and she's three months old now. I better stop drinking, I'm starting to swear a lot. That's my signal.*

But she poured herself another big glass of wine and gulped it down fast. *Fucking lesbians. Why don't you go stare at yourselves and leave my baby alone.*

She couldn't stand lesbians either, ever since college when they were the cool girls and she couldn't make friends with them because she was straight and she didn't pretend to be gay like all those other girls who shaved their heads and wore T-shirts that said *Dip Me in Honey and Throw Me to the Lesbians.* And they were no more gay than she was, they just wanted to hang out with Shane and Astra and TJ and Chickie—God, she couldn't believe she remembered all their names, those smoky girls with their tiny undershirts and tattoos and pierced everything, the girls who ran the literary magazine and the theatre, the girls who were going to do BIG COOL IMPORTANT things with their lives, you just knew it.

"We should leave," said Kelly, behind Jane and Leanna. "This is ridiculous. We had a reservation. I'm going to grab pommes frites off somebody's table if I don't eat soon."

"We'd have to start waiting somewhere else all over again," said Leanna. "And it's ten now. Lots of places stop serving. I say we charge up those stairs and force the hostess to deal with us. We're too nice. That's our problem."

Jane thought, *I am too nice. That is my problem. All my ex-lovers leave me for women with nasty mouths who make scenes in restaurants. And yet they stay together. They leave me and they stay with the nasty ones. This is an important clue to the mystery of my love life.*

The hostess came tiptoeing down the stairs with a tray of wine glasses. A server followed her with two open bottles of wine. They poured very full glasses for Jane, Leanna, Kelly, and the other women in their party. "I promise," the hostess said. Leanna, dazzled by the free wine, flirted with her. "Oh, you promise all right," Leanna said. "You're a big promiser, aren't you? How 'bout delivering on that promise, babe?" The hostess laughed and poured her more wine.

Jane did not want to drink any more but she was so hungry she thought maybe the alcohol would take the place of food for a few minutes. She gulped down the glass and held it out for a refill.

The restaurant seemed to get louder and now it was fun to be standing elbow-to-elbow watching other people eat, great to be out on a Saturday night with a crowd of good-looking women like herself. *We are SO not losers,* Jane thought. *This is proof. Look at us, in a fabulous restaurant enjoying ourselves. Take that, ex-lovers.* She hoped they were all sitting at home wearing sweatpants and stuffing their fat behinds with pizza and beer, utterly bored with each other and their lives.

The mother of the baby thought the lesbians had a lot of nerve. They were getting louder and louder and she couldn't hear what her friends were saying. The whole restaurant seemed to be screaming but all she could see was mouths flapping and she was left out of the conversation. She turned to her husband but he was busy telling a long, funny story to his friend. The baby was getting restless. She made an *ack-ack-ack* noise and wriggled and kicked her legs. Her husband put his hand on the baby's cheek and stroked her absentmindedly, like he was petting a cat.

"Stop it," said the mother. "Give me my baby. Don't pet her like she's a cat." She stood up and grabbed at the baby. Her husband kept hold of the baby and gave her a gentle raised eyebrow, one of those married-people looks meant to convey, *Dear, you're getting a little out of hand, sit down and knock it off.*

She glared at him and sat down. Don't give the lesbians more to stare at. Look at the parents of the bearded baby fighting in public. Look at them tossing her around like a hot potato. Suddenly she wanted to go home. She felt drunk and angry and surrounded by strangers. But the lesbians were clogging up the aisle. She couldn't see any way to get past them until they were seated.

Jane saw the exchange between the parents, heard what the mother said. She sympathized totally with the father. *When you love someone, you love everything about them,* she thought. *You love their hair, you love their smells, you love everything that makes them what they are.* She thought it was sweet that he touched the baby's beard. You need to touch her like that so she knows in her bones that she is perfect.

Jane remembered sitting in her grandmother's lap when she was little. Her aunts, her mom, her women cousins would be talking around the kitchen table and her grandmother would be listening and laughing and smoothing Jane's hair. She remembered the bliss of being touched with love and being surrounded by the women who loved her and she smiled at the baby's mother as if to say, *Hey, lighten up, you have a good guy there,* and in that instant the mother stood up and threw her fork at Jane. She dodged it and it landed at her feet.

"Don't smile at me," the mother said to Jane. "Don't look at me and don't smile at me." She picked up a knife and pointed it at Jane. "You people."

It seemed to Jane that the restaurant hushed instantly. The servers froze mid-service. The hostess stopped dead on the stairs. The other diners stopped eating, forks halfway to their mouths.

Jane said, "I didn't do anything." She looked around at the room full of strangers who looked like they expected an explanation. "I didn't do anything to her. I was just standing here." But in her heart she knew she had done something, something bad. She was guilty. She had pointed out the baby to Leanna like the infant was a freak show and not a little girl.

"You smiled at me," said the mother, aware now that she sounded blurry even to herself. She tried hard not to be so drunk, to crisp up her diction. "Keep your fucking smiles to yourself. Nobody wants you here. You're clogging up the aisle and you're too loud and I'm sick of you looking at me. I am really sick of you." The mother seemed to get a head of steam going the longer she talked. Now she slammed the knife down, stood up, pushed the table aside, and squeezed out next to Jane.

God, I wish I could let loose like that, thought Jane. *I have never told anyone what I really think of them like that. I have never ever made a spectacle of myself in front of strangers. I have never thrown anything at my lovers, no matter how much I felt like it as they walked away, ripping holes in my heart.*

Jane didn't have time to be afraid, it was happening so fast. The mother bumped up close to her in the crowded space. She smelled the wine on Jane's breath and the lemon shampoo in her hair. She saw Jane's black bra in the gap between her shirt buttons. She thought *Why don't lesbians ever let me be their friend? Why do they have to congregate in groups and push women like me away? Why can't I go out drinking and dancing and having fun and doing cool things with them?* She swayed a little, dizzy and dreamy, thinking of herself as a college girl again, no baby, no husband.

Jane touched her on the arm to steady her. She saw the three of them—mother, father, and little bearded baby girl—walking home later together to a house full of toys and happy noises and baby smells. She wanted to say something important to the mother, something to touch the anger and soothe it away, something to make it all right.

"There is no one," Jane said. "I have no one to shoot me a look." She nodded towards the woman's husband. "No one who knows me so well she can just look at me and I know exactly what thought she is sending me."

"I hate when he does that. He drives me crazy," said the mother.

"Lovers. What are you going to do," Jane took a chance and smiled at her again, because Jane was a nice woman and nice women want to feel good and they want others to feel good and a smile usually doesn't incite people to throw forks. A smile usually makes people smile back. She wanted to feel that being threatened with utensils was an unusual response to a smile and very unlikely to happen again.

The mother leaned even closer. She liked the steadying feeling of Jane's hand on her elbow. *Wheee, I'm a little dizzy*, she thought. She liked the confiding tone of Jane's voice. She forgot why she originally came over to Jane and what she was going to say. She felt like she was at a party and had met someone new to talk to while her husband was off in another corner. She said, “We haven’t had sex since the baby was born. I’m not really thinking of him as my lover lately.”

The other diners resumed eating, some of them looking up regularly to make sure nothing violent was going to happen. Leanna and Kelly and the other women made their way toward the hostess on the stairs, edging away from Jane and the mother. Jane heard Leanna say, “We’re coming up, babe, ready or not,” and they all clattered up the stairs towards the hostess, turning to gesture to Jane. She waved back to them that she’d be there in a minute.

“That’s easily fixed, isn’t it?” Jane said. “You could have a naughty tonight. You could go right home and fix that, couldn’t you?” Her Aussie crept out when she was buzzed. They both looked over at the father, who was dressing the baby in her coat and hat, getting her ready to leave.

The woman laughed and swayed a little more, “He’s so proper he probably wouldn’t. He’d say it’s more beautiful and special when you’re sober or some shit like that. And I am not sober, that’s for sure.”

“Take it when you can get it, that’s what I say,” said Jane. “Not that I do.”

“You’re kidding, a beautiful woman like you? What’s wrong with these women?” said the mother.

“You tell me. It’s all a big mystery to me,” said Jane. She liked being called “beautiful” even if it was from a straight woman. Lesbians at her age, in their 40s, with a few ex-lovers under their belts and bruised hearts, reminded her of shy dogs who needed a lot of coaxing before they’d stop ducking and shaking when you put your hand out to pet them. She was like that too. But she wanted a woman like an eager dog, a woman who got excited to see her, a woman who got in the play position and stayed there.

The restaurant got loud again. It was late now and everyone had drunk a lot of wine. Jane felt like she was leaning on a bar, having a great conversation with a stranger, one that she wouldn’t remember later no matter how hard she tried.

"You know what I really, really, really hate. He handles me. He is sitting here right now handling this situation from afar," said the mother.

Oh, what the hell, Jane thought. She took a deep breath. "You know what I really hate," she said. "A woman who doesn't appreciate that she has everything. A woman who has never been so lonely she could eat her shoes."

"What does that mean?" said the mother. "You're that lonely?" Her husband approached, holding out the baby. The mother opened her arms.

"Yes. I am very, very lonely," said Jane, and the simple fact of saying the words out loud shook something loose in her heart. *I am very, very lonely and there's a table full of women waiting for me upstairs and they are ripping bread apart and dipping it in olive oil right now and ordering lovely risottos and gorgeous salads full of special little treats and when dessert comes, we will all share the sweetness and I swear that before the night is over, I will sit on someone's lap and lift her hair to kiss her neck and I will feel bliss again. I will.*

So Many Women, So Little Time

"YOU HAVE hooves," Trina said.

"Hooves as in . . . ?" Dee said.

"Animal feet. Look at those toes. You need to have your hooves trimmed," Trina said.

This is what becomes of letting exes move back in. They feel perfectly free to comment on the state of your toenails. *I could give a seminar,* Dee thought. She was a gracious old butch, a Southerner through and through. Trained from birth not to match an insult with an insult. Even an egregious attack on her innocent toes.

"Darlin', how about another margarita?" Dee asked.

"You drink too much. You have hooves and you drink like a fish." Trina was spitting now and *fish* came out a little slurred.

Dee went over to the bar, revved up the blender to remix the margarita batch, and brought the pitcher over to the poolside table. She filled Trina's glass right up to the brim. Take that, you old so-and-so. Trina scowled but she took a big gulp.

You used to be so nice to me, Dee thought. *You used to sit on the blazing hot sidelines of my softball games and hand me cold beers every inning. You cooked everything I loved to eat—gooey macaroni and cheese, chicken fricassee, shrimp and grits. You held my hand as we fell asleep at night. You'd whisper in my ear the parts of me you loved the best. My swoony eyes, my cootchie, and my hard little butt. Remember?* Dee looked down at Trina, who was staring out at the ocean.

"I can't stand you," Trina said. "You end up rich and you don't even deserve it. We were poor. We struggled. Now you live like a freaking rich person."

It was true. Dee used to play this little game with her money back when she was working, first as a Phys Ed professor, then as a corporate sports consultant, back when it was all heady fresh stuff, when a new breed of hero women with incredible muscles and sweat running down their faces suddenly towered over America on billboards and shone on front pages of magazines and in advertising all over the world and inspired girls to run, jump, train and no one made fun of them anymore, no one called them tomboys. Dee helped make women athletes rich and famous. And she got rich too.

While Dee was riding the wave, the game she played was buy-a-little-house, sell-a-little-house, like those little green houses in the Monopoly games she and her sissy used to play when they were kids during the endless afternoons of their Georgia childhood. She believed in real estate, not stocks and bonds, not gold bars. She didn't study the real estate market or follow any plan. The houses got bigger and bigger.

She followed her instincts, unloaded one when she felt like it, and bought another couple when she felt like it. She kept her big pot of money secure and made a side pot of money to play with. Both her pots doubled, tripled, went crazy every couple of years. The old folks in her family had a saying, "Money goes where money is," and it happened exactly like that, her money sucked more money to it like a big old magnet.

So now Dee lived in a sumptuous oceanside house of glass in Miami Beach. She had a housekeeper and a cook and a gardener and she hadn't worked in years. She loved silky linens on the bed, perfect tasty meals that appeared like magic, wines so good you had to groan at the tiniest sip.

Trina glared at Dee. Dee squatted for the pure pleasure of feeling her body work. She pumped herself up and down like she was powerlifting at the gym. Brown and sculpted, Dee's legs were one of her very favorite parts. And her arms, with their bulging muscles and firm curves, stopped strangers in their tracks.

Dee loved the open fascination she got from both men and women. She wore sleeveless shirts to show them off no matter what the temperature. *What the hell, I do believe I am in the best shape of my 63-year-old life.*

"You never loved me, did you? I know that now. I was an unwitting bit player in the continuous dyke drama of your love life," Trina said.

Now, see that's why I liked you in the first place, thought Dee. *I love a woman with a good vocabulary. Who says unwitting?*

Dee felt she owed it to Trina to listen as Trina carried on. She had acted like a dick to Trina, it was true. She had cheated on Trina often and with blatant enjoyment, came home whistling. In her heart, Dee thought that if she didn't promise monogamy, you couldn't be held to it one iota. To the best of her recollection, Dee had never promised her anything more than lovely times when they were together.

But Trina was romantic and delusional like every femme Dee had ever known. When Dee said *I love you,* Trina turned on the magic femme translator so what she heard Dee say was *I love you forever, I choose you for my very own, forsaking all others.* What Dee actually said was *I love you*, meaning *I love you this minute, I love how you smell, I love what we just did to each other's bodies, I love being a woman-loving woman.* That's what they used to call themselves, dykes and women-loving women and lesbian separatists and family, most of all they called themselves family. *Is she family?* they'd ask, meaning, *Is she one of us?*

Trina started to cry now, tears trickling down her face, shoulders shaking. The water in the infinity pool they sat beside moved to an invisible edge, overflowed, and returned. It was hypnotic to watch the water slide over the edge again and again in a little ripply waterfall. The ocean was a spectacular backdrop, waves rolling in, sun on the verge of setting with orangey, purply streaks leading the way toward sunset. *Well if I have to be tortured by an ex,* Dee thought, *at least I can enjoy my view.*

Trina sobbed. She blew her nose on a cocktail napkin that read *So many women, so little time.*

Dee couldn't think of one dang thing to say. She patted Trina's leg encouragingly.

"Don't pat me like I'm a dog," Trina cried. "You're the dog. You're the dog who ripped my heart out and feasted on the ruination of my dreams."

Dee quickly removed her hand. "What can I do for you, sugar? I'll do anything to make you feel better."

"You can't do anything now. You did everything already."

Many moons ago, Dee thought. Apparently there was no statute of limitations on the betrayals of lovers. She wondered if Trina was losing it. Why bring all this primordial junk up now?

After Dee and Trina broke up, Trina had gone on to live for many years with another woman, a stolid, dependable gal. Not a heck of a lot of fun, from what Dee heard, but faithful as a coon dog until she died. Trina and Dee were frozen in time back in the 70s, with bad haircuts and flannel shirts, marchers in countless protests, making love under a blanket on the back of a bus after everyone else was asleep on their way home from a reproductive rights march in DC. Or was it an Equal Rights Amendment march? They were always marching in those days for some damn cause or other.

Dee had been stunned when she opened her front door two months ago and saw Trina there with a hefty suitcase, after being out of touch with her for decades. Still beautiful, her body lithe and trim, only her white hair, funky orange and lime glasses, and a few crinkles in her face showed her sixty-something age.

"Well, come right on in, honey bun," Dee said, and Trina had moved in, just like that. Now Trina was living in the first guest bedroom.

Did Trina need money? Was that it? Dee had no problem whatsoever writing her a big fat check. Last time she heard, though, Trina had a house back in New Jersey and still worked as a massage therapist and yoga teacher. Dee was too polite to ask about Trina's job or house or finances. She was afraid Trina would think she was hinting for her to leave. When Dee was growing up, relatives moved in and out of their house in Georgia all the time, and nobody poked their nose in to inquire too closely. It was simply not done.

Maybe Trina sold her house and quit her job because she was bored or lonely. Maybe she got downsized. Could a yoga teacher get downsized? Was there a glut of lavender-wielding masseuses on the market? It was really none of Dee's business.

Trina stood up unsteadily. "I don't know what I'm doing here. I never wanted to be one of the army of your ex-lovers. I said, if she doesn't want me, I will cut her right out of my life forever. I'm not going to be one of those lesbians all enmeshed with their exes. It's sick. It's wrong. It's not me. You know it's not me," she cried, clutching Dee by the shoulders. "But here I am in your guest bedroom, lined up with all your other exes. I hate it. I hate myself for not leaving. You know what I see when I look down the hall? The woman you left me for. Then I walk a little farther down and I see the woman you left her for. You keep all your exes under your thumb here. It's disgusting beyond belief."

Dee wanted to say, *It's not all my exes, not by a long shot. And I didn't invite them to live here. They showed up, just like you did.*

As if magically summoned, Hawk Ann and Millie appeared in swim suits then, carrying appetizer trays and martini glasses. Dee's dog Jelly Bean trotted out from the house with them and sat at Dee's feet, smiling up at her. Dee beamed down at her sweet little face. *Oh, Jelly Bean, I adore you.* Jelly Bean's whole body wagged back.

"You see?" said Trina, pointing her finger at Hawk Ann and Millie. "This is exactly what I'm talking about. Your life is a big old party and all the guests at the party are your exes. That is so, so sick." She toppled unsteadily over and sat down hard on the patio tiles.

Hawk Ann slid down the curvy pool slide, shrieking like a grade school girl when she landed in the water. Millie jumped cannonball-style over the side, holding her knees to her chest. They splashed and carried on for a few minutes, then floated quietly, eyes on the coming sunset.

Dee wished she was a painter. She would give anything to capture the floating women, the purple and orange clouds hovering over the blue pool, its edge disappearing so that the women seemed on the verge of slipping over the waterfall into the ocean and beyond. It was all so beautiful and miraculous. A kid like her, from a dirt road in Georgia, ending up here.

"Even your dog is so super special," said Trina. "You can't have a regular old dog from the pound. Oh, no. You have to have a Havanese. A dog nobody ever heard of until five minutes ago. A movie star dog. The national dog of Cuba, of all places."

"Now look here," said Dee. "You can pick on me till the cows come home. But lay off my dog." She picked up her white fluffball and cuddled her like a baby. Jelly Bean whimpered happily, crooning her I'm-in-love-with-you doggy song, making Dee laugh out loud.

Trina screamed, "Children are STARVING in Somalia right this minute. What RIGHT do YOU have to live like this?"

Hawk Ann and Millie swam to the side of the pool and hung over the edge watching, but they didn't get out.

Dee put Jelly Bean down carefully and took Trina's arm, forcing her to stand up. "Trina, you are all mixed up right now. You're mad at me and you're sad about the children and you need to go in now and settle down."

It wasn't hard to steer Trina inside. Screaming seemed to have drained all the angry out of her. Dee led her to the house, opened the doors, gently pushed at the small of her back, and closed the door hard behind her.

Hawk Ann and Millie looked at Dee expectantly.

"The thing is, she's absolutely right," Dee said. She knew there were people who were blessed and people who were cursed. She had ended up on the right side and she didn't know how or why.

The sun hovered close to the horizon. The women turned to watch the irresistible spectacle. Without taking their eyes off the sun, which shimmered and bounced as it sunk lower and lower, Hawk Ann and Millie gestured to Dee to get in the pool with them. They stood together chest deep, arms around each other's shoulders.

Dee felt an immense gratitude for her beloved friends. How lonely life can be. How sad that moment when the lover leaves, that click of the door closing her from your life, the empty bed, no smell of her, no clinking of dishes in the kitchen, no burbling laugh, no sound. It didn't matter if you were the one who left or the one who was left, it felt really, really bad.

Hawk Ann rested her cheek on Dee's cheek. *But they come back sometimes*, Dee thought. *When the anger is gone, when the hurt ebbs, the lovers come back as exes. They forgive me. I forgive them. We start again.*

The door opened. Trina pulled her suitcase outside and walked to the poolside. Her face was red from crying and she didn't look Dee in the eye when she spoke.

"I'm so terribly sorry. I don't know what got into me. You have been nothing but kind to me," Trina said.

Jelly Bean bounced her way over to Trina, like she had just arrived from a faraway place and they were all seeing her for the very first time in a long time. She barked her happy excited bark. *Welcome, we're thrilled you're here, we love you, we all love you so much.*

"Don't go," Dee said. She got out of the pool.

"I'm like a crazy cousin," Trina said, "who shows up uninvited to the party, drinks up all your booze, and insults you on top of it all."

"Pretty much," Dee said. "But we don't hold it against you. We've all got a crazy cousin inside us, truth be told."

Trina stood there for a long time looking at them all before she picked up her suitcase and left.

Dee was shocked at how much it hurt, how the sound of the car starting punched her right in the heart. She let the pain die down before she turned and dove right back in.

Sissy

I HAD PLANNED on spending the holidays with a bottle of Chablis until my sister Mag showed up, itching for a fight. At the restaurant, she switched tables three times. The first table had no view, she said. It's nighttime, there's nothing to see out there but blackness, I thought, but kept my mouth shut. The second table was too cold, she said. I'll give you that, I thought. The whole place, one of those touristy floating boat restaurants, was chilly and deserted. It looked like it had been shut up for months and reopened halfheartedly for Christmas Eve. It smelled bad, too, like bilge water was sloshing below the floor. The third table had a wobbly leg and was too sticky, she said. By now, I was mortified but I slid out obediently and followed her to table four, where we stayed.

"I'd like to hear your specials," she said to the waiter, leaning forth expectantly, momentarily pleased by all the table-switching.

"There are none," he stated flatly, handing her a menu and stalking away.

"Well, for crying out loud," she said to his back. Turning to me, she said, "What kind of a joint did you bring me to?"

It was eerie to look at her, an old lady with grooved wrinkles, pouchy eyebags, too-black dyed hair, and see those same glittering eyes that haunted my childhood.

"I was planning on spending the holidays with a bottle of Chablis," I said. "Don't blame me. I eat at home or at Captain Shrimpy's on special occasions."

"That rat trap. That ptomaine pit," she snorted. "I'm not going there."

"Well, here we are," I said. "Not there."

The waiter came back. Reluctantly, I thought.

"Chablis, please," I said. "Bring a whole bottle."

"Water with no ice and a tiny sliver of lemon," she said to him. "I thought you were sober," she said accusingly to me.

"I am," I said.

"Yet you sit here and order wine."

"Holidays don't count," I stated as authoritatively as I could. Or when your nasty sister comes to visit unexpectedly, I thought.

She kept it up all through dinner. She sent back her salad, saying it was too cold. It came back steaming and wilted, like someone had put it in a microwave. She sent back her Bearnaise sauce to be warmed up. The chef came out himself to explain that you couldn't heat it up or the sauce would curdle. She smiled coquettishly at him and pushed the sauce back.

"Heat it up a little bit then," she said.

"You fool," I said. "Don't you know they spit in sauce when you send it back. Or worse."

"You're the biggest ninny I ever met in my life," she said. "Afraid of everything."

Well, that did it. I swore I wouldn't fight with her. I vowed to let her fight with chefs and waiters and a cop, if she could find one, but not me. Not this time. But I did anyway.

"I've worked in restaurants. I know what goes on. You've never worked a day in your ding dang life. He's back there spitting in your sauce right this minute," I said. "So don't you ninny me."

That was the most I had to say to her in years. I stood up. The hell with the Chablis. I had another bottle at home.

"Please sit down," she said.

My eyes almost bugged out of my head. My sister didn't say "please."

"I need you to help me," she said.

I am seventy-four. My sister is seventy-eight. She has never asked me to help her, in all our years. She's helped me plenty—a big check to bail me out of jail after I set fire to my first ex-husband's truck; a bigger check to buy a divorce from my third ex-husband, the stinking louse; a plane ticket to New York, when I thought I had another chance at an acting career; startup money for two small businesses—a typing business right before everyone bought computers and started typing their own papers, and a dog-walking service right before I broke both legs in my own driveway and couldn't walk for a year.

Now my sister—the rich one, who spent her life selling and buying houses and stocks, accumulating a fortune in that mysterious way some people do, without ever seeming to actually work, just watching numbers multiply on paper, until they reached old age with a huge pile of money—needed me.

"I'd like to hear you describe your desserts," she said to the waiter who appeared, hopefully waving a bill.

"That would be chocolate ice cream or vanilla ice cream," he said. "Are you familiar with ice cream at all or would you like me to describe it further?"

"What a smart aleck. I can't take any more tonight," she said, slapping money down. "Come on, Julianne."

I added a crumpled five dollar bill to the table to make up for the piddly tip I was sure she had left him.

We walked along the semi-deserted promenade. It was Christmas Eve and we were in Southern California, in a no-name beach town, far from the Jersey shore we were raised in and the hoity-toity New York City suburb she lived in now. The ocean was shimmery navy blue and the stars were as fakely beautiful as an old Hollywood set. I love California. I feel glamorous there, even if I am a failed everything. In California, my feet never quite touch the ground. I sail along on my daily chores—no one special, one of many dotty old ladies—but I glide regally there, always a bit above the ground.

"Well?" I asked. "What's the story, Sissy?" She hated it when I called her that.

"Don't you dare laugh," she said, glaring at me.

"As IF." I put a hand to my chest, acting shocked. She hated it when I used trendy expressions.

"My son's wife Claudette. You know, the one I can't stand. The one who's always taking so-called adventure trips, dragging my son up mountains he has no interest in climbing or bicycling across countries he has never heard of. That one."

"A lovely girl," I said. "Full of spunk."

"She won't shut up about swimming with stingrays. The most wonderful feeling in the world. The most enchanting creatures. She goes on and on about how great it is to swim with stingrays, how I should really swim with stingrays, how much I would LOVE those stingrays."

My sister stopped, clutched my arm.

"I don't know what the hell is happening to me," she said. "I can't get the idea out of my head. I am absolutely dying to swim with those G.D. stingrays."

I laughed out loud.

"I told you not to laugh," she said.

"Do I listen to you?" I said. I was sparring to give myself time to think.

"You mean those big flat fish with creepy flappy wings and beady little eyes? The ones that look like flying saucers with tails? The ones, that if you step on them, sting you? Hence their name. The ones that circle people in a pack, brushing up against them to get food? You want to intentionally get in the water with those fish?" I asked. I get all my information from nature channels on television. Ask me anything about cheetahs.

She nodded, blushing like she was admitting to an affair.

"So swim with the stingrays," I said finally, shrugging.

"And give Claudette the satisfaction? She must never know," Mag said.

"So go by yourself and don't tell her. What's the big deal?"

"I can't do it alone. I need you."

It was exactly like all those times in childhood when she forced me to climb huge trees with her or go out in the ocean when the waves were slapping us all over the place. I couldn't believe it. Seventy years had gone by and here we were in exactly the same place. A leader and a follower. Except she never used to ask me. She used to make me.

"You are out of your ever-loving mind if you think for one minute I'm going to do any such thing," I said.

I was terrified of jellyfish and eels and other darting creatures under water, and she knew it. She watched me many a time run out of the ocean back in New Jersey, shrieking "Jellies! Jellies!" like they were men with machetes chasing me.

"Please," she said, staring into my eyes and clutching my arm. "I'll pay you."

"Money has nothing to do with it," I said. "How much?"

"A million dollars," she said. She looked dead serious. This was a woman who hated to part with a nickel.

"Put it in writing," I said.

So that's how we came to be on that boat the next day, headed out to sea off the coast of Baja, two old ladies dressed in bathing suits, for crying out loud, with floaties on our arms to keep our heads above water.

Mag had hired a man with a catamaran to take us out by ourselves, instead of going with a group. She didn't want anyone gawking at her or spoiling the moment by talking when the stingrays showed up. The boatman said they would come in a school of several dozen. He smelled like a long Saturday night in a dark bar.

"What happened to your legs?" I asked Mag, to put her at ease. She had a nervous beatific look on her face like she was going to a shrine in Yugoslavia where the Virgin appeared to a goat herder.

Her legs were swollen to twice the size I remembered. Her calves and ankles looked like sausage rolls ready to burst.

"I got fat, all right?" she said. "What happened to your breasts?"

"Over-use," I said, and she cracked up.

"What are we doing here, Sissy?" I asked.

The boat slowed, getting into position. The water was as clear and untroubled as a dimwit's eyes. We were alone out there, the two of us and the boatman.

"Who the hell knows?" she said.

"Really," I insisted. "What are we doing out here?"

"We're just going to see some fish, all right? Do you have to get so G.D. philosophical about everything? So California about everything? So what's-it-all-about-Alfie?" she mocked me.

"What are we doing here, Sissy?" I said. "I don't see you or hear from you in five years, then you show up on Christmas Eve and pay me a million dollars to put on a bathing suit and feed fish in the ocean?"

"I don't know," she admitted. "I heard about this and I knew I had to do it. It had to be you and me. It had to be the ocean."

The boatman pointed. He looked pained to be forced to talk. He instructed us like he was reading from the script of a TV show he had watched too many reruns of.

"Jump in," he said in a monotone. "Do not walk normally when you get to the sandbar. If any stingrays are on the bottom and you step on them, they will sting you with their barbs. That is quite painful. Instead, slide your feet along the sand, giving them warning. We call that the Stingray Shuffle." He paused as if waiting for us to laugh. We did not. "Stand on the sandbar. Hold out that bag of squid bait."

"Squid bait. It gets better and better," I said.

Mag and I looked each other over point-blank, at the wrack and ruin of our bodies. I could see past her body collapsing around her. I could see a skinny, flat-chested girl who kept up with the neighbor boys, the terror who dragged her fraidy-cat, little sister with her to jump the waves, who held me by the hand and made me walk out on our roof, who hoisted me over her shoulders to climb the cemetery fence late at night.

"I want my million bucks," I threatened her.

She laughed, took a deep breath, held my hand, and helped me splash out of the boat.

And there we stood, the two of us shoulder deep in blue, warm beauty, waiting for winged sea creatures to fly through the water to us. Arms open, we waited a long time, silently bobbing. The sun felt so wonderful on my head and face. When the creatures came rushing around us, we weren't afraid at all. We were ready.

Here's the Story

THE STORY I want to tell you is about a father who will die soon and a grown-up daughter who cannot call him or see him. She rides her bicycle farther every day trying to outrun the whole thing but she knows every detail, thanks to her sister who keeps calling to tell her it won't be long now, but still she doesn't snap to and run to see him. What do you say after years of silence when one person is dying? What do you say to get over so many hurts, even though they were little hurts, not big things like hitting, but things that meant to her that he didn't love her, didn't care if she were there or not, didn't care what happened to her? He went to work every day and brought home brown grocery bags full of food every week for all the kids and that was the extent of it. There were so many kids and we all wanted to crawl in his lap but we couldn't because he laid on the floor when he came home because his back hurt and he needed to be flat and then he fell asleep so that was the father-daughter relationship and when this daughter got As he blinked and said *good* but it didn't excite him at all and when she got a scholarship to college he blinked and said *good* but it didn't excite him at all and when she got into graduate school he blinked and said *I'm not paying for that* and she left home and never went back and didn't call him but went to see all her brothers and sisters and they loved her and were excited for her and their children sat in her lap and that made up for a lot but still her father remained a blinking mystery man to her who never gave her a goddamn thing except her share of the food in the grocery bags every week and now he was dying and she was supposed to go and say something, be something, feel something but all she felt was unable, unable to pick up the phone and say what, unable to drop by to see him lying sick and helpless and flat on his back again.

❦

It was a beautiful September morning. Her legs danced in anticipation. Here they came, mounting steadily up the hill to her house, the old men she bicycled with every day. She was forty and they were in their sixties and seventies, but they could outrace her, out-mile her, out-hill her any day. They rode fifty, sixty miles a day and their legs were muscled marble. Some had pot bellies, most had ailments, prostate or gallbladder problems, heart bypasses, cancer spots. But on a bike, they moved like silk, smoothly churning out mile after glorious mile.

Biking was all about putting in the time, racking up the miles. Up and down the hills until you hardly breathed heavy on the ascent, until balm spread through your body and soul and you went home happy.

She knew nothing and everything about the old men. They talked about wind, road conditions, routes. They didn't talk about their wives and children, the jobs they did before, money. But in ways that mattered, she knew them and they knew her.

They knew she was afraid of fast downhills and they let her go last, so she could brake if she needed to and not be embarrassed. She knew they were gentlemen, right down to the core, by the courtly way they moved her between them to protect her from the worst of the winds, and how they surrounded her when a dog chased them. They knew she was plucky and in love with biking, saw how she sparkled and lit up when horses behind fences galloped along with them, how she sang out goodbye after she finished her thirty miles and waved them on to continue another thirty or forty miles. They knew she was faithful to them, counted on them. She knew they were brave, tackling unknown roads and high hills with quiet determination.

She loved how they worked as a team, watching out for each other, voices calling out warnings and signals—*gravel on the turn, car back, HOLE*. Riding with them, she could relax deep inside.

When she was new, they saw how she struggled to keep up, always a few strokes behind, and they taught her how to draft behind them, to keep her wheel close by theirs, to ride in an orderly row that swept her up in their rhythm and made the wind flow around her instead of pressing on her chest, holding her back.

After a ride, she put on her professor clothes and went to work feeling happy and peaceful. Her life made sense. She thought about nothing troublesome, just what she wanted to eat and how sparkling the day was. Work passed effortlessly. Nothing bothered her until she got home and faced the blinking light on her answering machine.

❧

Everything hurt. Now he knew what his wife had felt before she died the same way, eaten up with cancer. She refused pain medicine because it clouded her mind. But still she came to a time when she didn't know them, not him, not the kids. He closed his eyes and felt again the panic. The baby couldn't even walk yet. *Don't leave me with all these kids*, he pleaded silently. But die she did and they picked themselves up and went on somehow.

❧

In the classroom, she assigned essays to be done on the spot, short ones. These were her problem students, the ones who had trouble writing. Her job was to teach them to express themselves, form clear sentences, and shape answers.

In between the standard topics, she slipped in new ones. Why do people have children? How old do you have to be before you are free? What is our obligation to others? The ones who didn't care about anything, the ones full of anger and cynicism, wrote back things that felt like private messages to her, bitter little truths laid out like a path on the paper.

It was a beautiful October day. Her legs danced with anticipation. Here they came, the old men cycling steadily up the hill to her house.

"Today I am not going to work. Today I am riding all day with you," she announced and she loved them for the quiet happiness that shone on their faces. "I decided to do the Australian Odyssey ride. Six months on a bike, starting in two weeks."

No one asked about work. No one asked about her family or who she was leaving behind.

They asked about every detail of the trip, what she had to bring and which parts of Australia she would tour and which bike she was bringing and how many other riders there were and the reputation of the bike company that sponsored the ride, until all of them were exhilarated.

Her father was supposed to die soon, any day now. Her brothers and sisters watched her carefully when they told her. She was the sensitive one, the smart one. They looked up to her. She was the one who went to college, then got more degrees until she became that exotic creature, a professor, a PhD.

She saw their eyes, knew she owed them a reason. She was helpless to explain. "I just can't go there. I can't," she said and her kindly family dropped the topic.

By the time she comes back from Australia, it will all be over. The passing, the funeral, and the grief will have rolled over the family and gone away.

She thought out loud about the other time, not meaning anything. "When Mommy died, he told me to stop crying at the funeral," she said, and it was as if she said he had molested her or some other terrible thing. Do not speak ill of the dead or dying, that was the rule she broke and even though the others didn't say anything, she knew.

"I am going to Australia for six months," she told them, as if banishment was her punishment, but she knew it was her salvation. She might as well have told them she was going to the moon. These people were rooted. These people had children to care for. These people were used to facing messes and straightening things out and going on.

The nurses told the family that it sometimes happened this way. A dying person gets to the lip of death and hangs there, for months or even years. No one knows why. He should be dead and buried by now. The nurses said the ones who don't die are waiting for something. They can't let go. The nurses told the family to go on with their lives. Other families gave up vacations, held off moving, and the dying one didn't die. *It's not good to change your plans*, the nurses said.

She was not prepared for Australia, for how hard and long the riding was, day after day. And no warm bed, no bathtub at the end of the day. Her thirty miles a day back home seemed laughable now, when they rode ninety miles a day or more in rough terrain.

The other riders were more experienced than she was. Some lived this way, bike bums riding around the world. Every day she prayed for endurance, every mile she concentrated like never before. Each revolution of the wheel, each lifting pedal stroke, each breath took everything in her for the first month. There were no thoughts of anything other than the ride; there was no looking at nature; there was only the pumping of her legs and the struggle of her breathing.

She was like a nun prostrating herself on the continent. She talked to no one except for necessities. She didn't call home and they couldn't reach her. No one helped her and she didn't expect them too. The only thing that could make her cry was the thought of her courtly old men back home riding without her. How they took care of her, how they shone when she talked to them about any little thing.

The first month was endless. She became a wild creature who knew only her bodily needs. Eat, ride, sleep until she toughened into some different being, a purer version of herself with everything extraneous burned out of her.

She rode easier the second month. Some days actually felt effortless. In her dreams, she continued to pedal. When she got off the bike at the end of the day, her legs felt strange, like they had been detached from her real body, the bike.

During her third month, she began to miss people. She pictured her six-month-old niece and how it felt when she went to sleep on her chest. A big sweaty baby asleep on her, she would give anything for that comfort right now.

Fourth month, she started crawling into the tent of a fellow rider at night, a man with smiling eyes who rode smoothly and calmly, not driven like some. They didn't talk about what they were doing. It seemed like a dreamy extension of the bicycling somehow, being too jazzed up to go to sleep right away and needing some other way to come down from the cycling high.

Riding became her life during the fifth and sixth months. That is, she forgot that she had another life before or anything to go back to. There was only the sky and the route that day and the abiding peacefulness. She could live this way forever, surrounded by beauty and journeying on alone. Food was her greatest pleasure and her only need after riding, filling the enormous hole inside.

When the Odyssey was over, she was stunned. She refused to use the plane ticket she had, postponed leaving for days until all the others had left and then she became resigned to going home.

❧

"He's still with us," her sister whispered to her at the airport. For a minute, she thought it was just a comforting saying. Gone and buried, but still with us in spirit. But no, she meant he didn't die after all.

"Come with us to see him. We think he's waiting for something before he can die. Maybe he needs to see you."

She let herself be led to the place where they had him, tied to a bed, shrunken into a crisp of a body, tubed and beeping.

"Rub his foot like this," she was instructed by her sisters, "they can feel things there." She fled the room with a roar, a wild creature who knew enough to run, to hide where no one could find her.

❧

The story that I want to tell you is about a father on his deathbed and a newly-purified daughter and how they manage to ride over a hill together, finally, once. That's the story I *want* to tell you, but it's not the real story, which is the one that ends with the father standing at the top of a big hill by himself looking down on all those kids and their kids and watching his life fly by, an amazing movie. There's a war and a girl smiling at him and a baby and another baby and a picnic and a graduation and another baby and a birthday party and it's all going by so fast and there's one of the girls on her first bike. Look at her go.

Salty and the Boss

SALTY'S HAIR was long and he liked it that way. He felt sorry for well-groomed men with short gel-shiny hair. He felt free of some regulation that they had to go by. He liked his messy, long, blonde hair. At work, he tied it back with a scrunchy ponytail holder like little girls wear. Every twist of his scrunchy was a little rebellion against the men in charge of the world.

Salty worked for a boss named C.C. It was an okay job. They didn't rig the timesheets. They paid overtime. Not every company did. Some acted like they were outside of wage laws and counted on their employees being too dumb or scared to know what was right.

At this company, they played fair and square with overtime too, spread it around so everyone got a crack at it. They even offered benefits but deducted money out of your paycheck for the health plan, so Salty didn't sign up. He needed every penny of his paycheck.

While he worked for the boss, three of his teeth turned bad and had to be pulled. But the benefits didn't cover this kind of dental work anyway. So he went to a dentist in his neighborhood who knew about poor people and he paid the dentist back a little bit every payday.

That paycheck was all his, no paying money for benefits that wouldn't help him anyway. Salty thought he made out good on that deal.

Salty was minimum-wage poor. He had four pairs of pants and six shirts but one of the shirts had stains and holes so he only wore that at home. He had two pairs of shoes, but one of them hurt him so much he limped if he had to wear them for more than an hour. But his good shoes were wearing out fast so he still wore the ones that made him limp, to save the good ones.

He had one heavy winter jacket and one hooded sweatshirt that said *Our Lady of Lourdes* on it. The sweatshirt came from the thrift shop and fit him perfectly. It was brand new and just warm enough for days when he didn't want to wear that heavy winter jacket and it only cost $2 so he didn't care that he looked like a Catholic wearing it. He knew that only homeless men wore jackets that were too hot for the weather, so he always remembered to switch to the sweatshirt so he wouldn't look like one of those godforsaken guys.

He wasn't homeless. He had a room in a house. After he paid rent on his room, he had $20 a week to eat from. So he went to the produce store where they sold a bag of bruised oranges and apples for $4 but you had to eat them fast before they went bad, so he did. He always hoped that those vitamins stayed with him until he bought another bag, because he knew his other food had no vitamins left in it. That's probably why his teeth fell out, from the couple days a week when he went to the McDonalds to buy $1 burgers. For lunches, he bought a loaf of bread and peanut butter for $5 and that's what he ate all week. If he worked overtime and had extra money, he went to Taco Bell and bought a burrito and nachos for $4 for dinner.

He craved salty stuff all the time. One time at work they asked him if he wanted some big chocolate-covered donuts the boss brought in and he said, "No, I'm salty," meaning that he craved chips or something salty and they all laughed and called him Salty from then on.

The boss had everything. A Bose radio. A big heavy Rolex watch. A black Mercedes with a special key that didn't even look like a key.

Two houses—one down the shore where he could hear the ocean while he lay in bed, and one in South Philadelphia, a sumptuous three-story townhouse on a nice quiet block where they said old Mafia guys lived.

The housekeepers in both houses were instructed to throw out all of the food every week, even the condiments, and replace it. C.C. and his wife hated old food. They wanted all new food in their refrigerators all the time.

The housekeepers took a lot of it home but how much mustard and ketchup could anyone use? So they threw out jars and bottles of things week after week. Anything opened had to go. That was the rule. The boss and his wife especially hated that black gunk that formed inside condiment lids. Growing up, their parents would never throw anything away unless it was used up and they told their children the black gunk was harmless but both the boss and his wife didn't believe that for a minute. The black gunk was gross and when they grew up, they weren't having any of it in their house. So the condiments were thrown out week after week.

The housekeepers bought food they liked, their favorite potato bread and Ben and Jerry ice cream flavors, because they knew they'd be bringing it all home to their house in the end. *These people eat out anyway, they never notice what's in the fridge*, the housekeepers said, and they were right.

Sometimes C.C. came downstairs in the middle of the night and looked in the refrigerator, but he rarely ate anything. He stared at the food. *Potato bread, I never heard of such a thing*, he thought, *my wife must like it. Phish Food and Chubby Hubby ice cream. For a skinny woman, she likes her ice cream.* He never wanted anything in there.

C.C.'s houses were full of closets with hanging shirts and $1,000 suits, so many that he didn't get to wear everything in either house. His clothes hung with tags on, stiff and new, many never even washed. C.C. didn't shop for his clothes. A woman came to the house and she measured him, her minty breath too close as she stood in back and wrapped her tape around him. He didn't like it but she was a good shopper and a week later, his last year's clothes were gone and his closets were filled again after she went to the expensive stores and shopped for him. His wife didn't want to shop for him. She told him she was too busy shopping for herself and men's clothes were boring.

His wife was skinny and hard-faced. She wore bright, slick lipstick that made her lips look like a chimpanzee's, he thought. She smelled bad under her arms and her mouth had fumes like sulfur. From not eating, maybe, C.C. thought. She was so skinny she couldn't get pregnant and that was okay with him. He didn't want children but you were supposed to, so he pretended to be disappointed. He didn't like having sex with her anyway and hardly ever did.

He had a mistress who had plump breasts that spilled out of her nighties and she smelled divine. Sometimes like French fries and sometimes like chocolate cake. She was an old-fashioned mistress who didn't mind taking money and liked that he paid her rent and bought her everything. She didn't want a job. She liked being his mistress. She liked having sex with him. He was so starved for touch by the time he got to her that she felt it was an act of charity. He didn't ask for anything fancy. She just had to lay there and open herself up. She felt beneficent with him. She figured she gave more to him than he did to her, poor guy.

But he gave her a lot. He gave her a huge sapphire necklace and dangling diamond earrings. He brought her bags of food from the Italian deli—mortadella, huge green garlic-stuffed olives in oil, gorgeous hard bread, and round balls of mozzarella cheese. He gave her a Mini Cooper, which was funny because she was so plump she had to wriggle into the tiny car, but she loved it. It was a fun car and she was a fun woman.

Salty walked most places. One day he stole a bicycle. Or maybe he didn't. Maybe the bicycle was a gift from God. He had walked by the bike in an empty lot on his way home from work. The bike was thrown down behind a bush, like a kid would throw down a bike and jump off to play a game with friends, then jump back on and ride home to dinner. He thought the kid would come back for it. But on day two it was still there, unmoved. So he covered it with branches. Day three it was still there, so he took it home.

He raised the seat and that helped to make it his. It was an expensive bike. It made a wonderful smooth humming noise when he rode it. It was fast, sleek, and thrilling and it made him so nervous to ride it. He was terrified the cops would pull him over and a kid would be in the car pointing his finger at him saying, "That's my bike, that guy stole my bike."

So he asked Smitty, the maintenance man at work, if he had any leftover paint. Smitty said he could have some red stuff, so Salty painted the bike red overnight. He felt a little better but he was still afraid to ride it much, after dark mostly.

He searched for a serial number on the bike and couldn't find one anywhere. *They hide them,* he thought. *They will pull me over and shine a special flashlight on the bike so the serial number jumps out, and they'll put me in jail.* He was very afraid of jail. *But the bike was just lying there, abandoned,* he cried to himself.

He worried himself sick over the bike and finally he got up at 3 a.m. one night and rode it back to the field and laid it back down, covered it up like he was burying a dog. It wasn't worth it. He went back to walking everywhere.

His job was a packing job. He stood in the same spot for hours and packed boxes at the boss's printing company. The boxes were full of glossy brochures for prescription drugs. The brochures were for anxiety, depression, stomach upsets, and erectile dysfunction. Salty had none of these problems. His penis worked okay. Every morning he woke up with an erection. He liked that. He got angry sometimes but not depressed or anxious. He saw no brochures for anger medicine.

Because of his job, his feet hurt all the time. He had bunions and corns. And his back hurt so bad. There was nowhere to sit down while you packed. It was definitely a standing job. So every break, he sat down immediately and stayed down. It was a hurting job, but it was a good job to him because they actually gave the breaks they were supposed to by law. Even if they had a rush job, they let people go to the bathroom or have a smoke.

The only things he didn't like about the job were his feet hurt, his back hurt, and the Spanish women never shut up. He didn't speak Spanish, never cared to learn. He didn't know what the hell they were talking about but they laughed and chattered constantly. He tried to pretend it was like any background noise and it was, in a way, like listening to airplanes overhead or a jackhammer because their talk had no meaning to him, it was pure sound. But he wished they would shut up sometimes, he wished he could hear silence. He was the only man on the packing line and he didn't know why, except maybe it had to do with his long hair.

The other men were printers, cutters, or printers' assistants. All the other men clumped together over there in the printing area, with their big machines running, running, running all the time and the assistants putting more paper in and grabbing off the printed paper when it came out. Mostly they spoke English over there. The cutters operated scary machines with big blades that could cut off a man's arm no problem. Salty woke up sometimes in the night with the sound of the cutters in his dream, a huge thwack, like a giant swiping down at him through the clouds, like a big arm knocking him into the path of an oncoming train.

The boss sat up front in an office with a big leather chair and a huge framed photograph of his father who had started the company and gave it to him. The boss could hear the hum of the printers and the thwack of the cutters and the chatter and laughter of the Spanish women. He could hear it all but it was faint and far away.

The boss sat in his office and wrote proposals for jobs to keep the presses running. His mistress called him all day long. She called him to tell him what she was watching on TV, what she bought at the store, what the neighbor said about the new neighbor, what her sister said about their mom. His wife never called. The secretary didn't approve of the mistress but the boss didn't care what she thought. She had no idea of his life.

The boss had gone to a big name college, Penn State, but he paid guys to take his tests and write his papers for him. He hadn't worried about school or grades or learning anything because he knew his father was giving him the printing company. He'd never have to send in his resume and wait for someone to hire him.

The boss hated that his father had put him in the big leather chair and left him there for life, like a big stuffed doll. But he was slow-witted and lazy. If he left this office, he'd have to get a job and he couldn't see himself standing in line begging for a chance, then working long hours to get ahead.

Salty showed up on time every day to his job. He never left early. He never asked for a day off. He was alone in the world so he didn't have to go do anything else. The Spanish women had to go sometimes. They had to go bail their brothers out of jail or take their kids to the emergency room. The other men at work had to take days off sometimes. For court, when they fell behind on their child support or were losing their licenses for drunk driving. To go to their kid's baseball tournament. To fly back to Puerto Rico to see their *Mamis*.

But Salty never had anything to do but go to work and go back to his rented room. So he never took off work. It was boring in his room, no TV, no radio. He'd sit on the front steps of the boarding house and watch people walk by, resting his feet and back until he got tired enough to sleep.

The best day at Salty's job was the day the boss came in with a huge cake, candles blazing. The cake said WAY TO GO, TEAM.

The boss said, "Thanks to all your hard work, we finished a rush job with an impossible deadline so now I am giving you a day off with pay. Have a piece of cake, go home early, and stay off tomorrow, on me," the boss said, not looking any of them in the eyes.

That was because his dead father was poking at him from inside, telling him what to say and do. The cake and the day off wasn't his idea. That's the kind of shit his father enjoyed, not him. But it was his father's company, and C.C. was his father's only son, so he did what he thought his father would have done, but he didn't enjoy it.

For Salty, though, it was a great day. His back and feet were so tired, he didn't feel like doing anything except resting, so he walked to the corner bar and watched the Phillies baseball game all afternoon, happily nursing two beers for hours.

The worst day at Salty's job was Halloween. The dead father who started the company had loved Halloween, so he had made a big deal of it. He started the tradition of having the workers dress up and parade in front of clients and vendors, who voted on the best costume. There was a $100 prize. They worked in their costumes in the morning, then at lunchtime they had the parade and a free catered lunch in the break room. C.C.'s father never dressed up, and neither did C.C. But the workers came as mummies and aliens and pirates. Some workers really tried to win, came up with clever printing-related costumes, like putting themselves into one of the boxes they packed.

But Salty and most of the men refused to dress up. They felt like someone was making fun of them. They stood with their arms crossed and watched the others march in front of the clients and vendors. Halloween was an uncomfortable day for the workers. Some of the more simple-minded ones did have fun, but most of them felt their pride was wounded and the costumes made them mad.

The company made a lot of money for the boss, year after year. He paid himself big bonuses at the end of the year, plus his big salary, which he got every month. But one month, when the boss added up the numbers, he didn't like what he saw. *We didn't make enough this month*, he thought. *This number is not big enough. My father wouldn't like this.* His father had been dead for ten years but still the boss constantly heard his father's voice in his head. *Who should I fire? A Spanish woman or a printing assistant? If I pay one less person, these numbers will add up better next month.*

He thought about the secretary but she seemed to be paired with his mistress in his mind because she transferred the mistress's phone calls to him all day long, every day. He stood up and walked down the hall, past the break room, and stared through the glass in the door that separated the machines from him. He saw the man with the long-haired ponytail who packed boxes with the Spanish women. *He has to go*, the boss thought. *I pick him.*

So when Salty got his paycheck that Friday, the secretary wouldn't look him in the eye but mumbled at him, "You got a notice in there. We don't need you anymore."

"What?" said Salty. He thought he heard her wrong.

She hissed at him, "It's in the envelope, open it up."

He opened the notice. *I'm fired*, he realized, feeling like he got punched in the stomach. "What did I do wrong?" he asked her.

"Nothing," she said. "Ask the boss."

So Salty knocked on the door of the boss's office and the boss looked up. "I was wondering what did I do wrong?" Salty asked. He really wanted to know. He felt anger but it was low down inside him.

The boss was afraid. He felt like a little boy whose father was mad at him. So he smiled very large, showing his teeth, and said, "You didn't do a thing wrong, it's just business is bad, that's all. Never mind, you'll get unemployment."

Salty said, "Unemployment's not enough, I need my regular pay and overtime to keep going in life. Unemployment's not much."

The boss said, "I'm sorry, maybe when business picks up."

"Your daddy gave you this business and you don't even deserve it," Salty said. He was picking up steam now.

The boss said, "Hey, watch it."

"Why me?" Salty said. "Why don't you fire one of the Spanish women who never shuts up or that pressman who came to work drunk last week?"

The boss said, "I'm the boss and what I say goes."

"You'll be sorry," said Salty, and he left. He didn't know why he said that. There was nothing he could do, nothing he would do to the boss.

But the boss picked up the phone and called the police. He said Salty had threatened him. He gave the police Salty's address. And then he told the secretary not to file the unemployment papers on Salty.

"He doesn't deserve it," said the boss.

"That's not right," the secretary said. "He was just upset. He never missed a day. Even when his teeth were pulled, he came to work bleeding."

"You shut up if you know what's good for you," the boss said.

"You have some nerve," the secretary said. "I could get ten jobs better than this one. And I wouldn't have to deal with your mistress all day long."

"Then go, you stupid bitch," said the boss.

"I'll report you for calling me that," said the secretary, and she got her things and left. She took her Christmas mug, her slippers, her hairbrush, her framed photograph of her baby nephew, threw it all into a plastic bag and left.

The police wrote up the threat incident but they were too busy with real crimes to go over to Salty's house about it. Salty lived in Camden, New Jersey, which had just made the national news as the murder capital of the US. So when they saw this baby threat, this nothing threat, the cops just filed it away. And they didn't even file it right into the computer system.

That threat disappeared in paper on some cop's desk and was swept away into a recycling can that was really just a waste can. There was no recycling, the cleaning company just put out special cans to make people feel better, like they were helping the environment, but really they threw the paper in with coffee grounds, banana skins, and tampons in the landfill.

That was a good thing Salty got, the gift of no arrest, no jail time. But he didn't even know about it. Salty had no idea the boss had called the police and of his narrow escape.

Salty felt very bad about getting fired. He knew he didn't deserve it. *Why me*, he laid awake, stewing about it. Those Spanish women yak yak yak and they were slow because of all the laughing. Sometimes they stopped packing to fix each other's hair. But Salty never did. His ponytail didn't require any fixing. He wasn't talking all day, laughing it up. So why did he get fired? And the other men, they had a hard time getting to work every day on time. They were hard drinkers and they cheated on their wives and their wives threw them out regularly. They lost their licenses and car keys and sometimes their cars. *Why me?* Salty tried to get over it but he couldn't right away.

Salty went to the unemployment office. They renamed it the employment office since the last time he had been there.

"Your papers aren't right," the clerk said. "Your boss didn't file the papers for you to get unemployment. You have to go back and get him to fill this one out. We have no record of you. We have no money for you until you get your boss to fill out this paper."

Salty went to see the secretary. He peeked in the door and she wasn't at her desk where she always was at lunchtime. She used to open her lunch and spread it out on a paper towel on her desk at noon every day. The secretary didn't want to eat with the Spanish women in the lunchroom. Or the Latinas as she tried to remember to call them. The printer men and their assistants ate out in back, on the loading dock, even if it was cold. They could smoke out there. So unless it was snowing or pouring hard rain, the men stayed on the concrete landing for lunch. It was noon and the secretary wasn't there.

One of the Spanish women saw him. "Where's the secretary?" Salty said.

"She quit," she said in perfectly good English and that made Salty mad. *These people, they don't want to talk to me, it's not that they can't.*

Why do they have to huddle together and shut other people out with their words, he thought. *That's just mean.*

"How do I get my unemployment papers signed?" Salty said.

"You have to ask the boss," she said. "No secretary anymore."

So Salty left. He was not going to go into the boss's office. He couldn't say exactly why but he knew he couldn't enter that office again and see that crisp man look at him with those narrowed eyes and big fake smile. *You fired me*, Salty thought. *Why would you smile like you didn't? I have no money now because of you.* He had $3 left from this week's food money and a $20 bill he had hidden away from himself for an emergency.

Salty was proud but not poor-white-trash proud. He wasn't too proud to do the work that Spanish people did, the hot work, the hard work. *Hell*, he thought, *I even did work the Spanish women did.* He was a worker and that thought filled him with happy feelings. He would find work because he was a good worker.

He walked until he saw a white man with a crew of Spanish men, shoveling a mountain of mulch around trees in front of a big house. "Do you need any help?" he said quietly to the boss.

And just like that, he was hired and ended up working again next to a bunch of people speaking Spanish all day. *What is it with me?* He thought, *I always end up with Spanish around me.* But these were men and they were quiet about it. They mostly spoke in short Spanish sentences and they didn't laugh that much. They waited until lunchtime to laugh and play tricks on each other, pulling each other's shirts up or putting a handful of mulch in someone's hat.

Here I am again, the only long-haired white man here, thought Salty. But he was crazy happy to be outdoors and be using his whole body and not just standing still on a packing line. He believed in saying thank you to God for blessings he received, so he did as he shoveled mulch into wheelbarrows. He got the hardest job of shoveling but that was okay since it was his first day. At the end of the day, the boss paid him in cash and told him where to show up the next day.

Salty counted the money as he walked home. It wasn't minimum wage, it was much less, but it was cash so he liked that. He had hated going to the check-cashing place with his printing company paycheck because they took some of his money away from him for cashing the check. He liked a pocket full of cash.

"Salty came to see the secretary about his unemployment papers," said the Spanish woman to the boss, back at the printing company. She was anxious to prove to the boss how good her English was. She desperately wanted the secretary's job.

The boss sat back in his chair surprised. "You speak such good English," he blurted out. "I didn't know you spoke English."

"Sure, no problem," she chirped. "I could help you out on the front desk if you like. I can type and do the computer work too."

"What should I do about Salty?" the boss said. His old secretary told him what to do with state papers and filling official things out.

"I don't know about that. I thought the boss handled that," she said. *Damn it. Why did I say that? Play along, act like you know what to do, stupid woman,* she said to herself.

"I don't know it right this minute but I can learn fast all about unemployment, no problem," she said.

"That's okay," the boss said. "I'll get someone else who knows what to do. You go back to packing, I guess."

"No, please give me a chance up front," she pleaded. She was breaking a rule and she knew it. No begging, act like it was coming to you naturally, act like you don't want it. Or they will never give a chance to you. She knew this in her bones but she didn't want to know it. Fuck these white people with all the money. *I have pride,* she thought. The boss said nothing.

"As you wish," she said, head held high, and went back to the packing line.

She wailed to her woman friends in Spanish, "That stupid prick wouldn't give me a chance." The women didn't stop working but they surrounded her with a stream of sympathy and told her stories about why she wouldn't have been happy all alone up there anyway, how they would miss her, how they loved her in the back and soon the woman felt much better.

The boss was so alone up front. He called his mistress. He never called his mistress, she called him all day long. She was surprised.

"My mother is here and my sisters," she said. "Do you need me? Why? What's happening?"

She was nice to him as always, but the boss was angry that he was alone up front so he said, "Never mind, don't let me disturb your fun," and slammed the phone down.

"My man is having a bad day, poor guy," she said to her mother and sisters. And she went on playing cards with them.

Something horrible started up in the boss's stomach. At first he thought the rumbling meant he needed to vomit. There was a rising up inside and a terrible taste in his mouth and his ears were ringing. It was so awful a feeling that he needed to kick something, so he did, the waste can, and it flew into the wall with a good bang. Then he flung his phone to the floor and stomped on it. He shook his fist at the photograph of his father but he couldn't throw it down to the floor even though he desperately wanted to.

I should spit on you, he thought, but he couldn't. He had no water in his mouth. *Daddy, I am tired of sitting in the chair you put me in. I am a man who wants to fling this door open and escape from this place. Everyone wants something from me here and I hate it. Salty wants money for not working and the Spanish woman wants a front desk job and my mistress wants to be left alone until she says come over and I don't know what my wife wants but she is never happy around me and I want things too but nobody cares what I want. I want to walk out of here into the sun and go somewhere else. I want more from life than this. I am alone and always alone.* The boss's eyes filled with hot tears and no one was there to see it.

Salty finished another day's work and had more cash in his pocket. The new boss liked him, he could tell.

"Dude, what'd you say your name was, Sugar? Sweety? No, it's Salty? Maybe we'll call you Chippy, like for potato chips," the new boss teased.

Salty laughed with the Spanish guys. See, they understand the new boss's teasing. They always do. They understand what is dished out to them, but they don't speak back in the language they are supposed to. They do their own thing all the time. *Just like me*, Salty thought, and he was full of a warm rising pride in himself that filled every vein. He walked home feeling like a king and smiling at his life.

You Are So Beautiful, to Me

THE DOOR salesman sat at Mary's dining room table. "Would you like to see my whippets?" he said.

Well, when you put it that way, Mary thought, *how can I resist?*

"Whippets?" she asked.

"My babies," he said, sliding out from his briefcase an 8" x 11" color photograph of three whippets, posed against a studio backdrop of snow-covered mountains.

I believe you came here to sell me a front door, Mary thought.

"They're beautiful," she said.

"I started with Daisy Mae, here," he said, pointing to the whippet in the foreground, legs stretched out in front of her. "I fell in love, plain and simple. So then I got Thor and he seemed lonely to be the only boy, so I had to go for Raymond. Whippets are amazing dogs. Did you know they're a cross between the Italian greyhound and the terrier? Not too many people are aware of that. So smart. They could knock your socks off, the things they know."

I can see that the door-selling job is just a way to have an audience for your whippet tales, Mary thought.

"Let me tell you what Daisy Mae did the other day," he said, leaning forward. "And I'll prove to you without a shadow of a doubt, that my little whippet is smarter than your average high school graduate."

"What school district?" she asked, thinking quickly. *I have got to stop this train.*

He blinked twice, fast. Then he launched into a complicated story involving false teeth, a baby rabbit, and a wheelbarrow.

Mary moved her eyes slightly to the window, watched the trees outside wave to her, first with one limb, then the other. The salesman's voice was a rollercoaster of tones, hushed and low during the dramatic parts, then high and loud for the denouement. She felt dreamy, the way she used to feel at Mass when she was a little girl, with her whole family beside her, all seven brothers and sisters, her parents at the end, family anchoring her to the pew, hemming her in tight so she wouldn't float up to the gold-rimmed ceiling with the angels and into the wide-open arms of Our Lady of Sorrows.

"You're a fool for those whippets," she said.

The salesman looked shocked. He didn't like being called a fool, even for love, she realized.

"I didn't mean anything bad," she said, laying her hand on his arm lightly. "It's sweet to see a man so wrapped up in his dogs." *I am making it worse*, she thought.

"I wasn't done with my story," he said.

"Oh, yes, you are," she said, getting up. She shuffled his door pamphlets and dog photographs, pushing their edges together in a neat stack. She was aware of her large breasts hanging near his head as he sat frozen, staring at her hands. She looked him right in the eye.

"My husband used to like to watch me ironing naked," she said. "I didn't care for ironing boards, so I'd lay the clothes right on the bed and lean over them. And my breasts used to bob and sway like apples ready to fall off the tree, waiting for a big windy gust to come along."

She paused for dramatic effect. His eyes were popping and his mouth hung open while he stared at her.

"And you know what," she said, "sometimes a big old wind did come along, you know what I mean, and knocked me right down on the bed!" She laughed then, and kept on laughing, even though it came out jagged and hurt her throat, as the door salesman grabbed his things, shoved them back into his briefcase, and ran out the front door.

"How do you like them apples?" she said, but she was talking to her husband in absentia, not to the whippet-loving salesman.

"A man came about the new door," she told her husband Jeremy over the phone. She tried to keep her voice light and casual. "He kept telling stories about his dogs until I had to put him out, like he was a bad dog himself."

"But did you buy the new door?" Jeremy sounded polite, distant. Like he hardly knew her. Like she was a nice neighbor instead of his wife of seven years. Instead of the woman he pulled down to the bed and to the living room floor, the woman he fucked so vigorously in a tent on a beach that it came crashing down around their heads.

She felt tears rising up through her throat. She started to shake.

"But DID you buy the DOOR?" Jeremy asked.

She slammed the phone receiver into the base, over and over again, as hard as she could, in rhythm with her sobs, then slid to the floor, flat out on her stomach.

"What did I do?" she screamed. "What. What. What. What. What. What." Until she realized she was staring at the door salesman's shoes.

She squinted up at him, her neck straining at the distance between them. Her eyes were nearly swollen shut. He was short, barrel-chested, his shirt open a few buttons down the front, gray and black hairy curls escaping.

"I thought you were being attacked," he said. "I came right in. I'm sorry. I thought you were being attacked. I heard this slam slam slam and you screaming." He backed away, toward the door.

Mary covered her head with her hands like he was the attacker.

"Are you going to be all right?" he said. "Can I call someone for you?"

Mary shuddered, her whole body undulating. She held her head tighter.

The man came back, sat down on the floor next to her, cross-legged like a swami.

"I can't leave you like this," he said. "I won't. No, sirree, Bob." He patted her shoulder.

He's like a burr, Mary thought.

He started to hum.

What in the name of Jesus? She felt foolish, like she was caught sitting on a toilet with the door open to strangers. Which really happened to her once in a trendy restaurant with a poorly-positioned bathroom and a malfunctioning lock. Except she wasn't sitting, she was squatting over it because she hated to actually sit on a public toilet. Even worse, to be caught squatting and aiming. A woman sitting at a nearby table took pity on her and shut the door.

"On top of Old Smoky," he sang. "All covered with snow. I lost my true sweetheart. From courting too slow." His voice was deep and rich, making her think of barbecued ribs for some reason. She could practically taste them, listening.

"When my whippets get upset," he stopped to say, "I often find that a song does the trick. They settle right down."

She rolled over to face him. "Stop. You and those whippets. What do they have to do with anything anyway? Singing to a crazy woman sobbing on a floor." Her face felt so peculiar, like it was cut in sections and some parts weren't working right. *My nerves are jumping right out of my skin,* she thought.

He waved his hands, like *See? It worked,* with a big smile on his face.

She pulled herself to her feet, patted at her clothes, fluffed her hair. She would have looked almost normal, except for the river of snot making its way out of her nose. She was the snottiest crier. All of her brothers and sisters added together could not have produced this much snot. And not a tissue in sight.

"Here," he said, slipping a cloth handkerchief out of his back pocket. At the sight of it, she almost started up again. Her father used to carry handkerchiefs just like that, and take them out for crying children, making them blow into it until they stopped. *Men don't carry them anymore,* Mary thought. *I haven't seen one in years, since my dad died.*

She blew her nose repeatedly, making a soft mushy mound in the cloth. *I'm throwing this out the minute he leaves,* she decided. *I will not have this snot in my washing machine.*

"Why did you come back?" she said.

"You're kind of far out in the country here," he said, getting up. "I forgot to ask you for some water for my whippets. Not sure how far it is to a store. I was going to give them a drink from your hose if it was okay with you."

"You brought your whippets here?"

"I bring them everywhere," he said, with an I-dare-you-to-comment stare. "I'm retired, really. They're used to me being around all the time. So today I said, 'Whippets, we're going for a ride in the country' and they got all excited."

"A retired door salesman?" Her brain felt sluggish from the Jeremy encounter. She was talking to this man, she could hear her voice, but she was still hanging back on the phone hearing Jeremy's new, careful voice in her ear.

He waved his hand. "It was my company, but I retired and gave it to my son. So I just help out now, when he gets busy. If I feel like it."

"I'm not buying a door from you." She felt like she had to make a stand somehow.

"I could care less, lady," he bowed from the waist, like a hero in an old movie. "That's the beauty of retirement."

"But I will give you water," she said, feeling a Lady of the Manor mood sweep over her. "Come out to my backyard."

"Meet you out back in a jiff," he said, heading for the door, and she remembered her dad saying that, making rhymes to make the kids laugh (*or my name ain't Biff*, Mary finished it for him). *Back in a flash, with the cash*, he'd say. *See you later* and all the kids would scream back, *ALLIGATOR*. Even the older ones couldn't resist. *SEE ya, wouldn't want to BE ya*, he'd say, grinning.

Her dad sang, too, in the car during long car trips. *Where in the world were we going?* Mary thought. They were always crammed into that car, going somewhere. *I've been working on the railroad, all the live-long day*, he'd start, and they'd all join in. The boys would change the words instantly, *I've been furking on the hair road, all the bingbang day*, messing them all up until the song fell apart about halfway through. *Cranapple juice drink, YOU STINK, cranapple cranapple juice drink, YOU STINK*, the boys sang butchered lyrics to commercial jingles out the windows at passersby. *Bad, bad boys*, her mother would say, *Albert, don't we have the baddest boys in the world.*

"I am going a little crazy," Mary said, watching the whippets run in and out of the sprinklers, frolicky as three-year-olds, wide doggy grins on their faces. She started to cry again.

It was very peaceful in the backyard. They were sitting in wooden Adirondack chairs, the kind where you were forced to lean back and your neck relaxed until you felt like a floppy-headed baby. *He has nice, hard legs for a man his age*, Mary thought. Those shorts were quite attractive on him, too.

She herself was wearing the same thing she had been wearing for four or five days, a summer dress that was her favorite work outfit before she came home that day and found Jeremy waiting for her. She stunk.

The door salesman threw a ball to his dogs, then another, pulling them out of his pockets.

"You are so beautiful to me," he sang to his whippets.

Mary pictured a new front door, the finishing touch on their four-year renovation project. "We made it all the way to the last item on the list. It had been so hard, like running a race for years. The minute we finished, we were going to have a baby." She felt dizzy suddenly. Then she blacked out.

The man patted her face with his hands dipped in cold hose water. The whippets came over and licked her arms with gentle little licks that felt so good it gave her the shivers.

"They're good in a crisis," he said. "Would you look at that? They know something is wrong. They know and they are trying to help."

She looked up at the tree canopy. *A person should feel peace under those trees*, she thought. There is nothing more peace-inducing. The trees, big old sycamores with fat gray trunks, swayed like old elephants over her.

"I have shame," she said.

"Wrong. Wrong. Wrong." He slapped his hand on the chair arm.

"He has killed me," she said.

"You need to eat," the man said. "When was the last time you ate? Not eating at times like this makes you a little crazy."

Mary couldn't remember eating. She knew she fell asleep on the couch a few times in the last few days. She knew she drank some water and went to the bathroom because she remembered the empty side of the medicine cabinet, staring at the places where Jeremy's toothbrush and shaver and jock itch powder used to be.

The door salesman went into the house. She heard him opening the refrigerator and cabinet doors. After a few minutes, she heard the ding of the microwave and dishes clattering. He started humming a jaunty tune. It sounded like "How Much is That Doggie in the Window?" to Mary, but maybe she was back in her family's childhood car again in her mind. They used to sing that one, too. The boys sang *How MUCH is that BABY in the window*, and punched each other in the belly, seeing which one would be the baby, which one would break, cry, and tell on the puncher.

Why am I remembering all this junk? Mary thought. *If you paid me a million dollars, I couldn't have come up with any of that before Jeremy told me he was leaving me. Who cares what the boys sang in the car? What does it matter if I can feel my sisters' skinny brown legs thrown sideways across my bare legs? That I can smell and taste the potato chips and caramel corn that we passed around twenty years ago?*

The whippets sat quietly by her side. *I feel guarded, like royalty*, she thought. They were clearly listening, ears cocked, eyes alert. What's going to happen? She wondered.

The door salesman came out with a mug of tomato soup and a peanut butter sandwich. He looked pleased with himself. The whippets sniffed the air but didn't move toward the food or beg, like regular dogs would have.

"Oh, food," Mary cried, "look what you made me," overcome with longing for the hot liquid to slip down her throat, dying for the peanut butter to stop the pain in her stomach. She ate fast, holding the sandwich with two hands like a squirrel.

He brought out more of the same things twice before she was finally full.

"What's your name, anyway? And why are you being so nice to me?"

"It's only right," he said. "I'm Sal."

She reached out and held his hand, all three whippets staring at her touching him, all six eyes concentrating on his hand in her hand, and she felt like they were all part of a circle, everyone here to help her and feed her and watch over her.

"If you're such a good guy, Sal," she said, "leave me a whippet when you go." She didn't mean it. She didn't even like dogs that much. She didn't have enough energy to feed herself or take a shower, let alone feed a dog and clean up after it.

He looked at her wide-eyed, jumped up, slapped his side as a signal for the dogs to follow him.

Why did she say such a thing? Maybe this nasty mouthy streak is what drove Jeremy away from her? Maybe he wanted to have a baby, but not with her, because she was such a smart-alecky woman and he wanted the mother of his child to be a nice smiley keep-your-mouth-shut simple woman.

She'd never know because Jeremy wasn't talking. He just said he had to go and that was that. *I'm not into this anymore*, he said.

"Stop, whippet guy," Mary cried. She forgot his name that fast. "I was only kidding."

He stopped, walked back, the whippets following along quietly, seriously.

"Lady," he said, "there are some things you just don't joke about."

"I don't know what to do," she said, to hear the words out loud.

"You need to call someone now," he said. "Carry on with your life." He sounded impatient. It was an order, like heel or roll over or play dead.

She was floating. *No one knows*, she thought. *It isn't real until someone knows*. If only she could stop going crazy, she could wait it out.

The man whistled for his dogs, turned back to Mary at the edge of the yard. "Call," he said, pointing at her.

"Sure thing," she nodded. "Will do." *You and what army will make me*, she thought, waving him away.

She sat back down and closed her eyes and stayed that way for a long time. Later when she told the story of her divorce, she always started with the whippets and the stranger who appeared to sing her up off the floor. It was a killer story; men and women wept openly and that's all you can ever hope to get from a divorce, isn't it?

Once Upon a Time

THERE WAS a boy who came to stay in the Children's Room of the town's public library. It was summertime so other children came in and left all day long, their arms full of books and DVDs and craft projects they made in storytime and summer reading club. But this boy came every day and didn't leave until the library ladies turned out the lights at 8 p.m.

A bony, white kid, maybe 10 or 11 years old, with long red hair hanging in his eyes and freckles all over his face, sat at the table that was supposed to be for the littlest kids. He opened a book in front of him and hunched over it all day and night, occasionally turning the page, his legs sticking out from under the table all scrunched and crooked. He didn't talk to anyone. When the library ladies asked him his name, he wouldn't look up or answer them.

Edith, the front desk assistant, reported to the new librarian, "He didn't eat lunch. He didn't eat dinner. Again. A hungry child sitting in here for hours on end—what are you going to do about it?"

Edith thought it was outlandish that the town had to hire a librarian with a Master's Degree in Library and Information Science to be the library director. They claimed they'd lose state aid funding if they let a non-librarian run the show. *I guess my thirty-five years here don't amount to a hill of beans,* Edith thought. Well, if this Murph the librarian with a name like a Labrador Retriever, with her crazy chopped-off hair and tattooed legs, was who they wanted, she might as well earn her keep.

Murph said, "What do you suggest, Edith?" She knew what Edith thought of her. It was clear in her pursed lips and the way she rolled her eyes at everything Murph wanted her to do, like ask people, "Did you find everything you were looking for today?" Edith acted like Murph had asked her to frisk people or dance a hula dance on top of the bookshelves.

"I don't have an advanced degree," Edith said, staring at Murph over the rim of her eyeglasses. "I'm sure I'm at a total loss. But I know something must be done. This is unacceptable."

Lots of things were unacceptable to Edith. Litter on the trail around the lake she walked at lunchtime. Divorce. The rate at which her hair was falling out. Flavored mayonnaise. Tube tops on large women.

"I do have an advanced degree, it's true," said Murph. "So I guess I should be able to solve the social ills of our entire society with that. I'll get right on it."

"There's no need for sarcasm," said Edith, pleased to get a rise out of Murph. *The perfect ending to a perfect day*, she thought.

"I'm dead serious," said Murph. "My degree should help me run a dinky little town library and figure out how to help a neglected child, at the very least. Or my name isn't Murph." Which it wasn't really. She just liked the name Murph.

"Well, tomorrow is another day," said Edith. She gathered her things around her, her insulated lunch bag and the cardigan that she wore like a shield against the air conditioning.

"Sufficient unto the day is the evil thereof," Murph agreed. She liked old sayings and clichés. Murph was thinking of what she'd eat when she got home. Something stinky. A big, old, red onion and gorgonzola cheese sandwich. Or tons of garlic and oil over pasta. She didn't have a boyfriend right now, which sucked except for these little plusses like not having to worry about bad breath.

"What?" said Edith. "Who said anyone was evil? I never called you or that boy or anyone evil. For the record."

"Good night, Edith," said Murph. She knew better than to try to straighten out a conversation with Edith once it went off the tracks.

"Even if that boy stole my lunch, I wouldn't call him evil. Everyone deserves three meals a day."

"Yes, well, good night, Edith," Murph tried again. She needed Edith to leave so she could set the alarm.

"Good night, Murph-y," said Edith. She loved coming up with little twisty, tormenting things she could do to Murph, things she could never be called on, like adding a "y" to the librarian's precious made-up name.

First thing next morning, the boy was back. Edith and Murph watched him go to the Children's Room and take his position.

Edith kept her eye on him as she checked in books with a steady, plodding rhythm. Hold it under the sensor, hear the beep, put it on the book cart, pick up another. It was the most satisfying dance in the word to her. The simple beauty of it. A person's record cleaned with each beep. A new start. Last week that woman thought she wanted to learn beekeeping and she took out three books but they sat there accusing her until she gave up the thought. She lives in an apartment, for God's sake. Where would she put a beehive? Now she's taking up knot tying.

Edith felt she kept people's lives straightened out, saved them from a lot of foolishness. She approved of libraries. Think of all the guilt-producing book buying that would happen without libraries, all the stacks of hobbies people never learned, all the money tied up in hardback novels that derided you silently when you couldn't get through them. The public library was the best recycling machine in the world. There was no commitment with a library book. But buy the book and it silently mocks you day after day. You still haven't traveled to Tasmania or adopted a macrobiotic diet? Where's the boat you were supposedly building in your backyard? Have you mastered taxidermy in six easy steps? Edith couldn't stand staring at her own mistakes like that and she couldn't imagine how others did.

Murph sat at her desk facing the front door. She hated her office, felt too disconnected in there even though it had a glass front and everyone could see her and she could see everyone. So she dragged a little desk out by the front desk and put a laptop on it and sat there every day, right near Edith.

Over the beep beep beep of the checkin sensor, Edith said, "So what's your plan? This cannot continue."

"I could call the Department of Youth and Family Services. But they take kids away if they think they're neglected or abused. Then they end up in foster homes and sometimes that's worse than the original situation," Murph said.

"He's right there, he'll hear you," said Edith. Why didn't the woman use her office, for God's sake? She thought Murph made a spectacle of herself sitting there, hopping up all the time and walking around bothering people, asking them if they found what they were looking for and if they wanted her to order anything specific. She acted like it was all about the library users, like they could have anything they wanted. Foolishness to the nth degree. There was enough nonsense on the shelves already. No one needed to read all those new things they insisted on ordering. Urdu and snake handling and goat farming and biographies of people you never heard of.

"You're right," Murph said and she went in her office and closed the door. She liked to throw Edith once in a while by obeying her. In the office, she picked up the phone, aware that Edith was staring at her. *I have to do something. At least look like I'm doing something.*

She called her best friend, Mary Margaret. Mary Margaret was a librarian too, but she worked in a rare book room of a large research university, a universe away from a small town public library.

"What are you doing, MM?" Murph tried to keep her voice low and her body language like she was talking to a town official, a nun, a suicide hotline, or something else super serious.

"Writing a grant for a digitization project, major bucks, nasty deadline," Mary Margaret said. "What are you doing?"

"I have this kid here all day every day. He doesn't seem to eat. I don't know what to do. Should I report him to someone? Feed him myself? What do you think?"

"Fuck if I know," Mary Margaret said.

"Come on."

"I mean it. I have no earthly idea. Don't you have a security guard who can eject him or something?"

"Mary Margaret, he's just a little kid. Jesus. I want to help him, not throw him to the wolves."

"What wolves? They have wolves in New Jersey?"

"You're so literal. You wouldn't know an expression if it bit you in the ass," Murph said.

"Dude," Mary Margaret said. "What do you want? Why are you ragging on me?"

"I'm just pretending to talk to someone. So Edith thinks I'm worth my salary. Play along."

"I have to go. Pretend you're a library director of a small town library in Southern New Jersey—hey, you are!—and make a decision already. I can't help you."

Murph made a raspberry sound into the phone, hung up, pretending to take notes from their conversation. She looked at the town's website in the Social Services area. It looked like a bunch of stuff for old people, Meals on Wheels and a Senior Center and a little bus for people with disabilities, and vouchers for food stamps. Nothing about kids.

A woman knocked on Murph's office door and opened the door. "The woman at desk say I talk to you. You the boss," she said, in an accent Murph couldn't place.

Murph was mesmerized by the woman's arms. They looked like scarred, gnarly tree trunks. This woman must wrestle alligators for a living. Her hair was dyed a strange purple black. She could have been forty or seventy and her shapeless gray clothes didn't help place her.

"Please come in. Sit down. What can I help you with?" Murph thought her own voice sounded bizarrely enthusiastic.

"My boy," the woman said, gesturing with her head to the boy in the Children's Room.

"That's your boy?"

"My boy sit here every day, all day, all night. I tell him come home. He won't come home. I give him bag with sandwich. He throw at me, won't eat. I don't know what to do," the woman said.

That makes two of us, thought Murph.

"He is bad. Like an animal."

"No," Murph said.

"He is the worst boy in the world. He is evil. Let him go hungry then. Throw food at me and I won't give you no more."

"He behaves himself in here. He just sits and looks at books. He doesn't talk to anyone, bother anyone," Murph said.

"I want you make him come home. I want you forbid him here." The woman slapped her hand down on the desk.

"I can't do that," Murph said. "I have no authority. It's a public place and anyone can come in here."

"Send for the authorities then. I am done," the woman said. "He make me look very bad. I am not bad. He is bad."

"Nobody is bad," said Murph. What the hell did she know?

"You take care of it. You're in charge now. You want him here, then you keep him here forever."

She's picking up steam now, I better do something, Murph thought.

"I'll go get the boy," Murph said. "We'll all talk. Okay?"

She went to the Children's Room. The boy saw the woman in Murph's office, and he cowered as Murph approached. She held out her hand and he took it. She led him to the office.

"You," the woman said, shaking her fist at the boy.

"Is this your mother? Grandmother?" Murph asked the boy.

He shook his head no. *Oh, good,* thought Murph. *This complete stranger comes in here and I let some defenseless kid go off with her, a total nutcase.*

"You lie. You are evil liar and very bad boy," the woman said.

He hung his head lower, like a sad little goat.

"Okay," Murph said. "Let's stop the name-calling and talking trash. Talk nice."

"You stupid," the woman said to Murph.

"Fuck you, you low-life bitch," Murph said. It was an uncontrollable response from her life before, when she was just a person and not a job title. When she could curse and push someone back if they pushed her, when she didn't have to act all professional and business-like all the time.

"Everything all right in here?" Edith popped her head in to ask, at exactly the right time to hear Murph curse.

"No," Murph said. "Everything is pretty bad in here. Nobody belongs to anybody. He won't eat the food she gives him. He won't go home. Like that."

Edith picked up the phone with a little sigh. *How can someone dial smugly*, thought Murph, but Edith did, looking exactly like the cat who swallowed the canary.

"Joe, please," said Edith and waited until Joe came on the line. *Whoever Joe was*, thought Murph. "Joe, can you come over to the library right now? We have a situation."

"Joe will be right over," Edith said, hanging up.

"The policeman take you and shoot you against a wall," said the woman to the boy.

The boy began to cry silently, his shoulders heaving. Edith put her arm around him.

"Shut your mouth," Edith said to the woman. "If you say one more word, I will duct tape your mouth shut. You understand me?"

The woman stared at her and said nothing. *Progress*, thought Murph, opening her desk drawer and handing a roll of duct tape to Edith.

A line of people waiting to check out their books began to form at the front desk. Edith glanced at them but made no move to leave the office.

Joe came fast, a policeman in full uniform with a smooth baby face. "May I have privacy please?" he asked, holding the office door open for Edith and Murph to leave.

"Shouldn't I stay? Representing the library?" Murph asked.

"No, ma'am, step out please."

Murph helped Edith check out the books of those waiting in line. Everyone seemed extra patient and tender with each other. They whispered, glancing over at the glass-front office and trying not to stare but watching the officer who leaned down to talk to the boy, who focused so intently on the boy that the boy started talking and crying. He talked and he cried and he talked and he cried and Joe listened to him and held out the tissue box to the boy. Then the woman started crying too and her face was beet red and Joe didn't give her a tissue. He held the office door open and she stepped out. She waited in front of the door and he made her wait there a very long time. He kept talking to the boy and the boy began to straighten up. The boy nodded at Joe, a little, tiny goat nod. He actually smiled, a tiny, little boy-to-man smile. Joe opened the door. The boy and Joe stood in front of the woman.

"Will go home now?" said the woman.

The boy looked up at Joe, nodded, and walked toward the front door. He stopped at the front desk.

"I'm allowed to come back whenever I want to read a book," the boy said.

Murph felt like she was going to faint. He could talk.

"That's right," Murph said.

When everyone was gone, Murph said to Edith, "Thank you. You knew exactly what to do."

"I wasn't going to tell you how to do your job. But then she came in here and I knew she was up to no good. I hate women like that. Like whoever that kid was to her meant she was allowed to say terrible things to him, things he'll never forget for the rest of his life."

"What a piece of work," Murph said.

"You said it," Edith said.

The moment of harmony was too much. The weight of it hung on their shoulders and they both wanted to start a little fight.

Edith charged, "You order too many copies of things off that *New York Times* bestseller list. I told you we don't need all that around here. Order one or two for the eggheads but don't order every single one. They're weird books. We don't like weird books around here."

"What exactly do you consider a weird book, Edith? I'd really like to know." Murph asked.

"I wouldn't dream of telling a professional librarian what to do. I'm sure I don't know half the things they teach you in graduate school."

Just then, the boy ran back into the library, stopped in front of Edith and Murph. "I ate my lunch already. I had a pickle sandwich and four cookies."

Edith and Murph looked at each other in amazement. The kid was talking again. Complete sentences. Like a little human being.

"Now I'm going to read a while. I'm allowed. Do you have any books I would like? Any books on like a pig and a dog and a boy all going on a trip? Or about pirates but not on a ship, in outer space? Maybe like a girl who beats up boys? Or like about a football guy. Or like a police dog and how he hunts down the bad guys. Or like—"

Edith interrupted him. "Settle down, child. Pick one thing."

"I want a book on how to build something out of wood and then a book on how to light a campfire and a one about a wild animal fight and Abraham Lincoln and Batman get together and they fight bad guys, like that . . ."

It was like someone wound him up and let him loose. The boy careened around the Children's Room talking to himself and then to a two-year-old girl who started running after him screeching and throwing books and taking off her shoes and throwing them, caught up in the mania the boy created. The little girl's mother chased her around the room. Then the boy jumped on top of the little table and waved wildly to Edith and Murph through the glass wall of the Children's Room before he crashed down, rolling on the floor laughing.

Murph hurried in to settle him down and then he pulled books off the shelving cart and tried to help her put them back, shoving them every which way and she said "NO" and it didn't slow him down a bit. Finally Murph got him to sit down by staring him directly in the eyes for a long time, like Edith stared at drunks and silly teenagers.

When she came back to the front desk, Murph was exhausted.

"Be careful what you wish for," Edith said.

They both broke out into that kind of surprised laugh that was really saying *I know I was wrong*. Edith laughed to say *Yes, I know I'm a know-it-all and it's really annoying* and Murph laughed to say *Yes, I have no idea what the hell I'm doing and I need your help*.

Murph said, "Geez, I hope she doesn't feed him every day. Look what happens."

As they laughed, the boy snuck up on them and pounced. "What's so funny? I like a funny book a funny movie a funny video game. Do you have a funny book a funny movie a funny video game? Are you laughing at this, at this, at this, at this?" and he pushed over a stack of books on the desk so they fell over, crashing down all over the desk, bringing down pens and signs and a vase with flowers from Edith's yard with them.

Murph pointed back to the Children's Room and he went, talking as he ran the whole way, throwing words over his shoulder like someone had pushed an ON button in his back, the little freckled evil boy, the boy who would not eat, the boy who had a hole inside from the woman who was or was not his mother or grandmother, from all the sad and terrible days of his life, so he didn't know how to stop talking, he didn't know how to play nice with other kids, he didn't know not to bother the library ladies, he just knew the moment his life changed when the library ladies stuck up for him and Joe the cop came to help him and now he was not alone in life and would never be alone again.

He's here and he's not going anywhere, Murph understood. He was her job. Managing him was her job. And there wasn't one single course she took in graduate school about him. *I know nothing. I need to take a class in poor little boys and how the library can be the place where they learn to be human. I need to read a book that starts "Once Upon a Time, a hungry little boy sat very still in the Children's Room and waited for Edith and me and Joe the cop to rescue him from the mean witch."*

Hawk Ann in Love

HAWK ANN lived in *slower* Delaware.

Fairfax wouldn't know slow if it reared up and bit her on the nose. She was like a little rocket, exploding all over the gay bar where Hawk Ann bartended.

"I bet you taste salty, girl." Fairfax grabbed Hawk Ann's suspenders and pulled her close, kissed her on the lips right in front of everyone.

Hawk Ann didn't like it. She wanted to court a woman properly, feel that slow heat grow until they couldn't stand to wait anymore, till they had to have each other or die. She felt incredibly bashful and odd, like her customers and friends and all the strangers in the bar had just seen her naked as the day she was born. Besides, she had met Fairfax only one hour before and didn't know a thing about her except that she had tawny skin that Hawk Ann was dying to touch and lips that tasted like Limoncello.

Slower, lower Delaware was dairy farms; foxes standing at the edge of fields at twilight; long back roads with treacherous ditches running alongside; pea soup fog mornings; abandoned school buses and house trailers with their windows punched out, rotting in overgrown patches of woods; hefty red-faced men fishing on the beach, their rods planted deep in the sand; horses in front yards; and children playing baseball near a canal where foul balls fell to the water floor and stayed there in the muck. Hawk Ann had been one of those kids.

But the inner circle of the area was also a prime tourist playland, with outlet malls, waterparks, and chain restaurants crammed up next to each other for miles leading into Rehoboth. The town was an epicenter for gay and lesbian tourists from DC, Virginia, Wilmington, Baltimore, New York, and Philadelphia. They came in droves for Pride Week, ManDance, Women's Festival, and Camp Rehoboth parties. They ate in gay-owned restaurants and cycled slowly around town on rented bicycles. They arranged themselves on rainbow towels at the women's beach and the men's beach, not officially designated as such but very clear to anyone walking by. Boy boy boy boy boy boy, girl girl girl girl girl girl.

Hawk Ann tried many times to hang out at the women's beach but she always felt like a German shepherd trying to curl up with frisky kittens. These visitors traveled in girl gangs. They rented houses together, roamed around town together, ate together, and most especially, drank together.

Hawk Ann could testify to the drinking. Friday nights, the women blew into the bar with whipped up energy they brought with them from their high-paying jobs where they thought fast and talked fast and did ten things all at once and if they paid for a beach house, dammit, they were going to throw themselves at having fun there, cram it all into one week or a summer full of weekends.

Once, when Hawk Ann was working, a woman planted herself at the bar, yelled at Hawk Ann over the music, "Take me out of here right now and fuck me silly," loud enough that everybody swiveled around and burst out laughing. Hawk Ann could have fainted from pure embarrassment. Plus she wasn't anyone Hawk Ann ever would have wanted to fuck. She was afraid of women like that, whose bones poked out from their skin. Too sharp, hard as a knife—Hawk Ann thought a woman like that might be the death of her.

But the woman was a steady customer, had been in every night for a week, blowing piles of money on pitchers of martinis with her friends. And Hawk Ann's boss was a jerk who watched her every move.

So Hawk Ann said, sweet as pie, "Sure thing, have one more drink while I finish up here." She knew giving that woman one more filled-to-the-brim drink was like knocking her out with a mallet to the head. Hawk Ann waited until the woman's eyes glazed over, watched as her head sank lower and lower and her forehead rested on the bar. And then Hawk Ann was nice to her, placing a bar towel under her head so she had a soft place to land. Even though the woman had been nasty to Hawk Ann, she couldn't be nasty back. Hawk Ann was just built that way.

This Fairfax was one of those grabby women, Hawk Ann could tell. One of those women who thought because she wanted something, she was entitled to it. Who thought because she was on vacation, manners and politeness didn't apply, that she could behave any old way and get away with it.

When Hawk Ann's boss stepped out back to smoke, Hawk Ann walked around the bar and over to Fairfax's table.

"May I speak to you?" Hawk Ann said.

Fairfax grinned up at her, then looked around the table at her friends like it was a little victory she won. "Did you come over here for another smooch?"

"In private, please."

Hawk Ann and Fairfax stepped into a corner. Hawk Ann kept her eye on the bar, watching for her boss. She didn't actually know what to say. Her mouth was stuck shut. She loved the lemony kiss but she was mad about it too.

Finally Fairfax said, "I'm sorry. I think I upset you by fooling around like that. I apologize."

It felt like the sun burst over the horizon to Hawk Ann.

"I get a little wild sometimes on a Saturday night," Fairfax said. "I swear you are such a hunky woman I got extra carried away. Please don't report me to the sexual harassment police."

"I will too," said Hawk Ann. "They have a special jail in town for women like you, who bother women like me while we're just trying to do our jobs."

Hawk Ann fell in love right then, hearing Fairfax's laugh. She felt that laugh all the way down her spine.

Fairfax asked, "What's your name anyhow?"

Hawk Ann answered, feeling that tinge of shame she always felt hearing the sound of her name. To her ears, though, Fairfax's name sounded like hands clapping.

"Hawk Ann," said Fairfax. "I'd appreciate starting over." She reached out to take Hawk Ann's hand.

"Yes," Hawk Ann stammered.

Fairfax raised Hawk Ann's hand and brushed her lips lightly to it. That did it, sent Hawk Ann over an edge inside herself, like she was running for the fun of it, no brakes, no fear.

They managed to talk a few times that night, Hawk Ann pouncing on every pause in the action at the bar to find Fairfax. At closing time, Fairfax was waiting for Hawk Ann by the front door.

Hawk Ann walked Fairfax home to her rental house in the Pines section. It was dark and quiet out, now that the bars had closed, and the women held hands all the way. Hawk Ann felt an immense happiness balloon out of her heart and bob around them as they walked.

They talked about playing Hide-and-Seek at night when they were kids, how wonderful it felt to scream into the dark when you felt that hand on your neck. Fairfax told funny stories about her friends in the beach house, stories that wound around exes and crazy affairs with co-workers and long distance love gone wrong. They fell silent when they got to her porch, tiptoeing up the steps.

Finally, Hawk Ann pulled Fairfax close and kissed her. It was amazing to feel Fairfax kiss her back the right way, like she knew who Hawk Ann was this time and she was giving her a little *Hello* message with her lips. Fairfax stood in the doorway grinning and waving goodbye before she finally went all the way in.

Hawk Ann deliberately didn't ask Fairfax what her plans were for Sunday or if she was in town for the whole week or for the summer. She didn't want to let her needy self out, that monster who roared and devoured everything in its path. She made herself stay in the present, no running ahead, no movie scenes playing in her head. This time, it wasn't hard at all. She was incredibly happy to splash around in the feelings she was having, to stay right in the warm happy bath of them.

She walked home holding her hand over her heart. Her house was on a street where only locals lived. No amount of money could turn these tiny, falling-down houses with cement blocks for steps and yards full of rusty grills and broken chairs into charming cottages for rent. But Hawk Ann was comfortable there, knew every sound in the night and every neighbor by name. She sat on her front step, not ready to go in and put an end to the night.

Her right toe was throbbing. Hawk Ann took off her work shoes, hard black Doc Martens that usually helped her get through a long weekend of bartending. Her feet were a mess. Bunions and corns and missing toenails. You'd think she was seventy-five instead of forty-five if you only looked at her feet. But if she wore the right shoes, they usually didn't bother her too much.

Now, her big toe was twice its regular size. *What the fuck?* Hawk Ann tried to remember if she had stubbed it or dropped something on it. She couldn't remember anything. She hopped inside and got a bucket and filled it with ice cubes and water, went back to the front steps to soak it. Her toe hurt like hell.

A police car slowly cruised by. Her friend Rocky leaned out the window. Rocky's real name was Rosa but she hadn't used that since ninth grade. "Hey, class act, what's with the bucket?"

"I met someone." Hawk Ann burst out with it.

"No shit." Rocky parked the car and jumped out.

Hawk Ann pulled her toe out of the bucket. It had inexplicably tripled in size, a sausage packed too tight in its casing.

Rocky and Hawk Ann stared at her toe.

"She's amazing," Hawk Ann said.

"That's amazing," Rocky said. "You need a doctor, dude."

"I would give anything to be with her," Hawk Ann said.

"I'm thinking emergency room."

"I'm doing it, man. I'm going for it with her," said Hawk Ann.

"WHOA, I think it's going to blow," said Rocky. "Come on, I'll give you a ride to the hospital. We'll turn the siren on and everything. You love that."

"I'll be all right," Hawk Ann protested weakly. She knew she wouldn't be all right.

"Right now," said Rocky.

The pain in Hawk Ann's toe intensified, like a torturer was holding a metal pincer on it and tightening the pressure. When she tried to walk, the pain stabbed up her leg all the way to her knee. Rocky held her up and Hawk Ann leaned heavily on her, trying not to cry. Every time Rocky braked on the ride to the hospital, Hawk Ann held her hand over her mouth so she wouldn't scream.

The emergency room doctor said, "My goodness gracious, what have we here." He fussed like a little old lady around her, propping her leg up and tucking blankets under it. He gave Hawk Ann an injection for the pain, but it didn't go away, just dulled it down a notch. A technician came in with an X-ray machine and took pictures. The doctor poked and prodded at her toe, muttered to himself, shook his head repeatedly. He gave her medicine for swelling, more painkillers, then he called in another doctor to look at it. Now two doctors were making frowning faces at it.

Hawk Ann was alone. Rocky had left after the first few hours to go back to work, saying she'd swing by later on to take her home.

Hawk Ann wondered if Fairfax was sleeping by now. Maybe she was dreaming of Hawk Ann. Maybe she would rush to the emergency room, come to her rescue because they were already tied together in a deep psychic way. Even in her delirious state, Hawk Ann stopped herself, begged herself to take one step at a time, stay in this place, don't go running down the lane into fantasy land.

Her toe was monstrous now. The doctors kept appearing and disappearing. The nurses injected new drugs into her IV. The pain was there but it was underneath the surface. Hawk Ann watched the pain, saw how it became an orange and purple pulsing thing, how it was part of her and separate from her at the same time. People talked to her, asked her things, and she couldn't answer them. She felt like she was trapped in a bad dream, the kind she used to have when she was a kid, where she was stuck and she couldn't scream, couldn't move. She lost track of night and day.

Rocky appeared out of the haze. Hawk Ann watched her mouth moving but she couldn't hear what Rocky said. She loved the look on Rocky's face right now. She tries to be so tough, but she's so soft and sweet inside. She's scared for me.

It reminded her of when Rocky would show up at Hawk Ann's house when they were kids, that awful house full of her ten half-brothers and sisters running amuck. You never knew what you'd find going on there. Like the summer the boys kept trying to fly off the roof. Three of them ended up with broken legs. The girls chased each other with hair brushes, frying pans, the hose—whatever it took to make each other scream and hurt. Hawk Ann was never without her baseball bat. She pinned the other kids against the wall with it and swung her way out of whatever came at her. It was an exhausting place to live and Hawk Ann hated it.

But Rocky's house was always the same. It always smelled of food cooking and it was full of happy sounds, like a baseball game on the radio or a TV laugh track in the background. Rocky had one mother and one father, not the parade of men that came in and out of

Hawk Ann's house. She had one brother and one sister, not a gang of kids who didn't even know who their fathers were. She had a normal mother, not one who named all her children for animals and birds like some kind of crazy person. She had a real mother, not like Hawk Ann's mother who acted like talking about being a great mother would make it true.

Hawk Ann could still hear her mother's gravelly voice, "I'm a natural mother. I love having babies, that's why I keep doing it. I can't help myself. I pop them out like nobody's business. It's what I was put on Earth to do." That's the kind of stupid shit Hawk Ann's mother proudly announced to strangers, to her welfare caseworker, to anyone who would stand still long enough to listen to her.

Half the time, the neighbors fed the kids, not Hawk Ann's mother. Rocky's mom loved Hawk Ann, gave her clothes and shoes and games, let her stay over any time, paid attention to her. Rocky was more of her sister than any of her real half-sisters. After Hawk Ann's mother died, hit by a car while wandering drunk on the highway in her nightgown in the middle of the night, her children scattered all over the East Coast and most of them didn't even keep in touch with each other.

Suddenly Rocky and her mom were standing over Hawk Ann. Their faces were so serious. Somebody must have died. Hawk Ann's thoughts anchored to that post, and she struggled to straighten up and listen.

"They want to amputate your leg," Rocky said. "Your whole leg, Hawk Ann. I don't know what to do."

Hawk Ann heard the words but they didn't mean anything. She was excited to see Rocky's mom. She had so much to tell her.

I met someone! She's amazing. Her name is Fairfax and I'm in love. Finally, for the first time in my life, I am in love. She's funny and beautiful and she gets me. I can't wait for you to meet her. I want to have you over to dinner to meet her. We'll have crabs and spaghetti, we'll have monkey bread, we'll have a barbecue, we'll have Easter eggs, we'll have clam chowder, we'll have chocolate cake with chocolate frosting, we'll have macaroni and cheese, we'll have beach fries, we'll have onion dip, we'll have every single thing we love to eat.

❦

It was nine months before Hawk Ann was out of the hospital and done with rehab. She was alive, that was the main thing. She had survived an incredible infection, a massive attack on her body from an unknown cause. Her leg didn't survive, but she did. That was the main thing. Everyone agreed.

She didn't remember much about the summer before she got sick. She didn't remember the night she got sick. And no one had the heart to tell her. It was only a woman she met in a bar one night. Nothing to mourn, nothing to see here, folks. Move along.

ACKNOWLEDGMENTS

The author gratefully acknowledges the journals where the following stories were originally published, some of them in slightly different forms:

"Hawk Ann in Love," *Cactus Heart*

"Bull," *The Kenyon Review Online*

"You Are the Bad Smell," *The Apple Valley Review: A Journal of Contemporary Literature*, nominated for a Pushcart Prize.

"Dip Me in Honey and Throw Me to the Lesbians," *The Barcelona Review*, nominated for a Pushcart Prize.

"Here's the Story," *Zone 3*

With immense gratitude to my teachers, editors, family, and so many loving friends who have encouraged and helped me along the way. Thank you to Autumn House Press for their commitment to independent literary publishing and for launching beautiful books into the world. Thank you to extraordinary writer, teacher, and friend Sara Pritchard for knowing, before I did, that my stories were ready to be a book. Thank you to my late parents, A.J. Anderson and Georg Ann Stowe Anderson, for raising a tribe of avid readers and good people. Thank you to public libraries, where the world opened up for me as it does for so many people. Most of all, a heartfelt thank you to my wife, Jackie, who takes me to the best places in life.

THE AUTUMN HOUSE FICTION SERIES

New World Order by Derek Green

Drift and Swerve by Samuel Ligon, 2008*

Monongahela Dusk by John Hoerr

Attention Please Now by Matthew Pitt, 2009*

Peter Never Came by Ashley Cowger, 2010*

Keeping the Wolves at Bay: Stories by Emerging American Writers, Sharon Dilworth, ed.

Party Girls by Diane Goodman

Favorite Monster by Sharma Shields, 2011*

New America: Contemporary Literature for a Changing Society, Holly Messitt and James Tolan, eds.

Little Raw Souls by Steven Schwartz

What You Are Now Enjoying by Sarah Gerkensmeyer, 2012*

Come By Here by Tom Noyes, 2013*

Truth Poker by Mark Brazaitis, 2014*

Bull and Other Stories by Kathy Anderson, 2015*

*Winners of the Autumn House Fiction Prize

DESIGN AND PRODUCTION

Cover and text design by Chiquita Babb

Cover photograph: Strand, Paul (1890–1976) © Aperture Foundation. Rebecca, New York, ca. 1923. Palladium print, 19.4 x 24.6 cm (7 5/8 x 9 11/16 in.). Gift of Marilyn Walter Grounds, 1989 (1989.1135). Copy Photograph © The Metropolitan Museum of Art.

The Metropolitan Museum of Art, New York, NY, U.S.A.

Author photograph: Burkett Photography

The text is set in Truesdell, a font originally designed by Frederic Goudy in 1930 for use in a quarterly journal for book collectors. In 1939, the original drawings and matrices were lost in a fire that destroyed Goudy's studio. The font was revived in 1994 by Steve Matteson, based on typographic material stored at the Rochester Institute of Technology School of Printing.

Printed by McNaughton & Gunn on 55# Glatfelter Natural